The Heartbreak Killer

The Heartbreak Killer

Pamela Proehl

Library of Congress Control Number:		2013904837
ISBN:	Hardcover	978-1-4836-1100-6
	Softcover	978-1-4836-1099-3
	Ebook	978-1-4836-1101-3

Rev. date: 03/28/2013

To order additional copies of this book, contact:
Xlibris Corporation
1-888-795-4274
www.Xlibris.com
Orders@Xlibris.com
88062

This book is in dedication to my two sons,
Westin and Connor.

Chapter 1

Rachel watched as the horror unfurled below her. Was she dreaming? No, it was too vivid. Was this really happening? Who was this maniac, and why did he want to kill this woman?

Raw, untamed fear surged through the woman's body like an uncontrolled storm. The man behind her was closing in rapidly. The freezing dense forest was riddled with sharp rocks and frozen fallen branches, bloodying her feet. In spite of the pain, she had to keep running—to do otherwise would surely be fatal.

When the woman looked back to determine how close her attacker was, she tripped over an exposed tree root and fell down hard onto the unforgiving forest floor. Excruciating pain shot through her ankle like an electric shock. Pure adrenaline was the only thing that enabled her to get up, but her quick sprint was now reduced to a slow, frantic hobble.

He heard her cry out. She was closer than he thought. The man behind her quickened his pace. The dark clothing he wore made him nearly undetectable against the blackness of the night. The only discernible clue that he was there at all was the reflection of the moonlight off the knife he was carrying.

"Oh my god. Run! Run!" Rachel cried out desperately to the woman below, but her voice was silent. She tried again, this time straining her vocal cords, but her warnings were mute. Why couldn't she hear herself?

Just as her voice had failed her, her ability to move was also impaired. What was blocking her? Was she in one dimension viewing into another? If it was a dream, why couldn't she wake up? Just as the woman trying to escape was helpless, so was Rachel—trapped and silent.

Suddenly, at warp speed, Rachel was inside the killer's mind. She could read his every thought and feel his every emotion. Rachel's thoughts raced in tandem with his, twisting and turning. It was like trying to rationalize some impossible maze.

The despair he held within himself was almost unbearable for Rachel to take. His grief covered her like a lead vest sealed to her chest, contaminating her soul.

"I am a gentle man, I am a kind man"—his mantra reverberated through Rachel's mind, over and over like a broken record. He didn't want to commit such a grisly crime, not again. The only comfort he felt was in knowing it was not his fault. It was his mother's fault. How could she make him do such horrible things to these innocent girls, knowing that a slice of his sanity was sacrificed with each life he took? He was slowly going mad.

Confusion swirled through Rachel's mind. It didn't make sense. First of all, he didn't have the mind-set of a cold-blooded murderer—there was no rage, no sexual intentions, no revenge driving him to do this. He really did not want to hurt this woman. Rachel could feel it in him. What was it about his mother that drove him to murder in the grisly manner in which he was planning?

"No . . . no . . . please don't do this!" Rachel hoped her silent words would penetrate into his mind—just as his thoughts penetrated into hers. "You don't

want to kill her—please!" Unfortunately, the only thought resonating back into Rachel's mind was that he would have his victim within seconds.

Finally, he was there. Reaching out from behind the woman, he grabbed a lock of her hair and pulled her head back toward him. She tried to jab him repeatedly with her elbow to free herself, but that made little difference. He kept a tight hold of her hair while turning her around. Although he had studied her flawless portrait a hundred times before, he was just as enamored with it now as he had been the first time he'd seen it. "You are a beauty—flawless," he said as she struggled against him.

"Please, please, let me go!" the woman pleaded desperately.

Every feature, every angle of her face had been branded into his brain. "Such a lovely face, exquisite in fact," he whispered, stroking her face gently with his gloved index finger.

Rachel, although hovering high above them, could hear everything that was said as if she were right next to them. It was crystal clear. It didn't make sense. How could she hear them so precisely when she was so far away?

"Please, don't make this difficult for me. I don't want to hurt you—at least not yet," the man whispered calmly, continuing to look into the woman's eyes, eyes that mesmerized him.

"Please don't hurt me! Please don't! I'll do anything! Just don't hurt me!" the woman screamed, struggling against him. At five feet seven with a slender frame, she was no match against him.

"Hush, my dear child, it won't hurt for long, and I will be here with you when you die."

Through the darkness, he could see the panic on her face. Her expression was that of terror, yet it was stunning to him at the same time. He wanted to look at her for eternity, but he couldn't. He had a job to do.

He gently eased her down to the ground. She reached behind her and grabbed his hands, trying to free herself, but the killer's hands were still cinched around her hair like a vise.

"Let her go, you bastard!" Rachel screamed, hoping her voice had somehow become audible and he would hear her. She desperately needed to break free so she could somehow help this woman.

The man pulled the woman to the ground. "Now I need to roll you over," he told her. "You see, I want to remember your face as it is now. Faces aren't pretty when they're dead."

With that, the woman cried out in terror. "Why are you doing this?"

Rachel tried to move her legs, her arms. She needed to get closer. She needed to stop this maniac from what he was about to do. But regardless of her determination, she couldn't dislodge from where she was perched.

"Now, c'mon, lie down on your stomach," he commanded, guiding the woman's face gently toward the ground. It was effortless, even though she continued fighting.

"I don't want to look into your face when you die," he explained. "You see, the first woman I killed was lying on her back and I had to watch her face as she died."

He remembered witnessing the face of his first kill and how it had been a monumental mistake. The dead cold eyes branded into his brain. They still haunted him. The horrific images demonized his mind, Rachel's mind. Rachel started to feel nauseous as she too saw the vision. The visions that consumed him, consumed her. They flipped over and over in his head like a bloody slide show, torturing him. His first kill had been more savage, messier. He didn't have the experience then that he had now.

"Please, listen to me, let her go! You don't have to kill again!" Rachel's mute words fell on deaf ears. Still, she carried on. "Don't do this. She's an innocent woman!"

He heard nothing. Instead, his thoughts shifted to the resentment he felt toward his mother. She was the one making him do this. As those thoughts entered into Rachel's mind, she wondered what was the significance of his mother, and why would she drive him to such insanity?

"Don't listen to your mother! You know the difference between right and wrong!" Rachel concentrated hard on her message. "Kind men don't kill. Remember? You said it yourself. You are a kind man. You can still walk away."

He didn't flinch. Unfortunately, the internal dialogue only ran one way. Instead, he spoke to his dead mother. "She is so innocent. You know how sorry I am for what I did to you. I know I deserve to be punished, but how many do I have to kill until you forgive me? How many before you can love me again?"

"Let me go! Please," the woman gasped.

He straddled her gently, easing the weight of his body down on to her, pinning her flailing arms with his legs. Gently, he ran his fingers through her hair—so innocent. Sadly, her stunning appearance would be her demise tonight.

"Oh my god! Oh my god! What are you doing?" the woman muffled, snow and dirt invading her mouth.

"*Dammit—stop!*" *Rachel scolded sharply as she watched him. This small, captured innocent woman was so frail compared to him. He eased up a bit, worried he was putting too much weight on her. He didn't want to hurt her. It wasn't time for that.*

Not yet.

He told himself there really was no sense in killing her. Not now, not ever. But the decision to kill her or to let her live was not his to make.

Finally, Rachel broke free from whatever was holding her back. Although she still couldn't move her arms and legs, she gently floated down to the ground right next to them.

"*Let go of me! You're hurting me!*" *the trapped woman screamed.*

"*Listen to her, you bastard! Don't kill her!*" *Rachel screamed, mere inches from the man's ear—still she was mute. Her paralyzed vocal cords ached with effort.*

Without any reaction, he continued. He unzipped a pack wrapped around his waist and Rachel watched him remove a red wooden heart, a white rag, and a black indelible ink pen. He carefully placed all the items next to the knife he had put on the ground.

"*I have to kill you now. If it were up to me, I would certainly let you live. It's my mother who wants you dead—not me.*" *His trembling voice betrayed him—sweat appeared on his forehead and his hands shook.*

"*Then let me go, please,*" *the woman begged, dirt-stained tears smudged her face. "Don't listen to your mom. You don't need to do what she wants!" Her voice remained loud, but her body was slowing as she tired from her struggle.*

"Yes I do. I did a terrible, terrible thing to my mother." His voice quivered like a small child who had just been reprimanded.

Rachel was ravaged with fear. She tried desperately to grab him, but she still couldn't move her arms. She was completely immobile.

The woman on the ground trembled. "Shhh, my little princess, you are just making this harder. If I could die in your place, I surely would." He put less pressure down on her now that she was weakening.

"Darling," he spoke softly, like a parent trying to comfort a child. "Like I said, I have no choice." He took one hand and began caressing the back of her head. Her hair was so beautiful, he thought. Then his fingers lowered to her neck—the very part of her body that would soon drain her from life. His heart quickened and he murmured, "I'm sorry, I am so sorry. Please forgive me."

Rachel stayed solidified, just inches from him. The full moon radiated just enough light for Rachel to study the man's face. The first thing she noticed was a scar that extended from his left eyebrow down to his lip. His face was broad, rugged, and ironically handsome in a unique kind of way.

Rachel focused on the deep lines etched around his eyes—evidence that he was most likely in his late thirties or early forties. She couldn't make out the color of his eyes—but they looked dark. A few dark curls fringed the bottom of the black knit cap he was wearing.

Not only was the man deaf to Rachel, he was blind to her as well. He made no indication that he saw her beside him. Rachel looked down at the woman. But because the woman was lying facedown, all Rachel could see of her was her blonde hair splayed out on the forest floor.

Rachel felt his breath on her face. "Don't do it, you son of a bitch!" she screamed again into his ear. His face bore exactly what he felt, what Rachel felt—sorrow, regret, guilt, torment.

"I've done nothing to you!" the frightened woman snapped out angrily. "Nothing!"

"I know you haven't!" he replied impatiently. Regretting his outburst, he sighed deeply to control his anger before speaking again. "You must not blame yourself. You can't help that you are beautiful."

The woman wept. "Don't cry, my darling," he said, using his fingers to root around for her cheeks. He wanted to dry the tears shedding from her eyes. "You see, when Mother was alive, she was a lot like you—young and beautiful." He used the back of his other hand to softly rub her cold bare arm. Exhausted, the woman just whimpered quietly.

"But she is dead now, and she doesn't want to be replaced." He paused and cocked his head to one side, staring down at the woman's lovely back sheathed in ivory. It was a sharp contrast to the backless black dress she wore.

"C'mon, you twisted freak. Let her go!" Rachel cried out, trying to swing at him with arms that still betrayed her. It was as if she were wearing a straightjacket.

"I still have to do what Mother wants," he explained to the woman. "If I don't, she will punish me. Please know that I am really a gentle and a kind man. I am not a monster."

His tortured soul died a bit more. "It's important to me that you understand this. You see, it is not my fault, and it is certainly not your fault."

Rachel felt resentment swirl within his mind—her mind. "My mother hates me for what I did, so I need to make it right. I need to let her know that I love her enough to kill for her—kill you for her. The only way I can regain her love is to kill for her."

He raised his head up toward the sky. Rachel saw his tears start to glisten. The salty liquid fell down his face, some pooling into the deep crevice of his scar.

Rachel felt the heaviness of his heart. It was as if it was breaking. She found herself even feeling a bit sorry for him. How could she? How could she feel anything other than disdain for this maniac?

Rachel had no power over him. All she could do was watch an innocent life be taken at the hands of someone who really believed he was a kind and gentle man. It was as if she was a mere observer of some horror flick.

Randall bent down to whisper into the woman's ear. "Please forgive me, my beauty, please. My heart breaks for you." The woman gave another futile attempt to free herself.

He reluctantly took a portion of her hair and pulled it back, exposing her fragile neck. He picked up the knife beside him and put the point of the knife underneath one ear.

He paused.

The girl gasped, trying to breathe.

Crouching down, he kissed her on the back of the head.

Although Rachel knew her arms wouldn't budge, she desperately tried to grab the knife. "Don't do this. She doesn't deserve to die!"

"Mother," he said, looking up toward the sky, "I do this for you." He then slowly sliced her neck from ear to ear, nearly decapitating her. The only sound that rose from the woman now was an eerie gurgling.

He hated that sound.

The neck that Randall had so admired just minutes ago was no longer innocent. Instead, it was a violent stream of pulsating blood that would, within seconds, claim the woman's life. He watched her hope shatter like broken glass.

"You bastard! You bastard!" Rachel felt the heavy sadness that overpowered him. She felt his soul slowly die . . . again.

Keeping his eyes closed, the killer placed the knife beside him and bent down, so his face was mere inches from the dying woman's face. "It's almost over, my love," he said, caressing her hair that was now beginning to matte with blood. He felt the rhythmic successions of her blood pulsate onto his face. "I will not leave you to die alone," he whispered. "I will consume your blood until you are empty. It is my sacrifice to you."

When the blood stopped, he rose up. Every portion of his face was covered with blood, except his eyes, making him look like the devil. He reached for the rag to cleanse himself. He scrubbed hard, as if trying to cleanse his conscience as well.

He put the red-stained rag down and picked up the wooden heart. He took the black indelible ink pen and twisted off the cap. He bent down over the heart, and using as much precision as possible, wrote "Forgive Me" on it. He paused to look at his own creation to make sure the printing was perfect, like a child might look when learning to write. When he decided it looked perfect, he picked up the heart and placed it on the ground, about a foot above the woman's head. He then raised the woman's arms and cradled it between her hands. Once the display met his approval, he put the cap back on the pen, grabbed the bloodstained towel and the knife, and placed them all carefully back into his pack. He stood up, took a few steps back, and remained still as stone for several minutes.

"My dear god, what have you done?" Rachel murmured. As if he heard her, he began to sob. For several minutes, Rachel cried right along with him. She was overcome with the savagery and senselessness of it all.

Finally, he looked up to the sky, spread both arms out as if he was about to pray for forgiveness, and spoke out loudly. "I hope you can love me now, Mother." Then he turned briskly and walked into the black abyss of the night. Rachel heard his weeping echo through the caverns of the forest.

Blood was everywhere—mixed in with snow, dirt, and leaves. Rachel's body finally cooperated, freeing her arms and legs. She kneeled down closer to the dead woman, whose head was turned to one side. The gash was so deep that Rachel figured if it weren't for a few sinews of flesh, the woman's head would've been completely severed.

Should she try to roll the woman over? She had never seen a dead person before, much less touched one. The thought made the putrid, sweet taste of bile seep up into her mouth. For a long time, she sat, contemplating what to do. Finally, she gently gripped one side of the body. She slowly turned the woman over on to her back, praying the head wouldn't come off in the process.

Rachel couldn't make out what the woman looked like because blood had seeped into every cavity of her face. It wasn't until after she used her shirt to clean off all of the blood that she saw the magnitude of the horror.

The moon cast out just enough light for Rachel to see the woman eerily staring back at her through eyes that could no longer see.

Rachel found herself paralyzed, not by the force that had immobilized her before, but by sheer terror at what she saw. Her body was not her own—it started shaking as if it was the epicenter of a horrific earthquake.

When she finally got her footing, she ran into the woods like an innocent animal sprinting from its predator. The howls that came from her lungs weren't human. The image of what she had just witnessed possessed her like a demon. She knew that face.

She knew it well.

It was her own.

Rachel woke with sheer terror pulsating through her. Dizzy from hyperventilating, she was soaked with sweat. It felt as if someone had just poured a bucket of water onto her bedsheets.

Dear god, it happened again.

The dream—she had it again.

She looked out her window and witnessed the same moon as in her dream. It eerily cast a column of light throughout her bedroom.

Chapter 2

Rachel Carter loved the view from her small condo. She lived in Kirkland—a quaint little suburb that rested on the eastside of Seattle. "It's as small as a Cracker Jack box," her mother would complain to her. Anita Carter didn't understand that, for her daughter, living in close quarters was a small price to pay for the panoramic view of Lake Washington that spread out across her second-story balcony. Rachel's place was her own little piece of heaven, and it suited her just fine. She preferred to refer to it as "cozy," not "small." It was eight hundred square feet with two bedrooms, a bathroom, a kitchen, and a living area that had a gas fireplace.

The furniture throughout the house was primarily whitewashed pine. She preferred the more "country" style décor just as her mother did. However, she didn't go quite as country as Anita. There were no wooden roosters cock-ca-doodle-doing from the tops of her cupboards and no border paper patterned with farm animals lining her kitchen walls. Instead of the powder blue carpet her mother had chosen, Rachel's was light beige.

Lake Washington was breathtaking. Every morning, Rachel's routine was to enjoy a piping hot cup of coffee while taking in the breaking of a brand-new day. She would often sit out on her balcony, weather permitting, and lose herself in the sailboats that swayed over the rippling waves.

She hadn't always lived in the Seattle area. Although she was born there, her family moved to Alabama when she was just a baby, so her childhood was spent as a true southerner. Hush puppies, grits, black-eyed peas, and catfish were the mainstay as far as good eating, and her mother sure knew how to cook them.

The Deep South was a friendly place. Everyone knew everyone, and everyone was always invited everywhere. Total strangers were greeted with the slow southern drawl of innocent hospitality. Among Rachel's fondest memories were the Fourth of July block parties. People from all around the neighborhood would flock to Mr. Huley's house. He was the main attraction because of his slow-churned, homemade ice cream. It was the best on the planet. Rachel would scramble, along with all the other kids, to secure a good place in line to get her red-white-and-blue cardboard bowl filled with the smooth luscious treat that slowly swirled in the metal canister.

Although shy, Rachel did have some good friends. Another favorable memory was of her and her best friend, Ronna Johnson, dancing on top of Ronna's bed to the tune of *"Crocodile Rock"* and *"Bennie and the Jets."* When they got bored with that, they would race out to Ronna's backyard and climb into the above-ground pool, where they were happy little fish swimming in a chlorinated sea.

Rachel's world came crashing down when she was just ten years old. Her mom and dad took her by her small hand, led her into the living room, sat her down and dropped the bomb. They would be moving to Washington state—something about her dad's job. She was absolutely devastated to leave her friends, her school, and all the things that made up her simple innocent world.

She didn't know much about Washington. Of course she knew the state existed, learning about it in school and all, but that was pretty much the extent of it. They packed the old 1964 Dodge named Rose Bud on moving day. Her mom drove Rose Bud, and her dad drove a big moving van up north and out west. Pretty much everything Rachel owned, as well as her parents' items, were stuffed somewhere between the two vehicles. When the car drove away from the only house Rachel had ever known, she looked out the back window. The tears that blurred her vision were maybe an indicator that she would never see Alabama again.

When her family finally arrived in Seattle, after a long and arduous trip, she concluded that she may as well have moved to a different country. Washington was depressing to her—an icky gray, gloomy, rainy place—nothing like the hot sun and blue skies of Alabama. People talked funny, but then again, most of the kids said the same thing about her. She was bewildered as to why people would wear shorts and tank tops in freezing seventy-two-degree weather. She may as well have been in the North Pole. Later, she realized seventy-two degrees was considered quite balmy for Seattle.

People in general were very different from what she was used to. They would glance at each other, but would make a strenuous effort to avoid eye contact. Saying hello to a passerby would constitute you as odd to most people. In Huntsville, Rachel knew everyone who lived in the vast spread of her circular neighborhood. In Washington, if your next-door neighbor acknowledged you, it was considered a small miracle. It seemed everyone pretty much hid within their own solitary lives with not much interest in anyone outside their own four walls. She gave them the benefit of the doubt. Maybe the weather conditions prevented them from hanging outside and having neighborly chats. It was strange.

On the first day of school, she was shocked at how the kids treated their teachers as well as each other. Although she wasn't sure then what the word was that explained the students' behavior, as time went on, she learned the word was *disrespect*. They swore, they raced around like wild monsters, and never seemed to listen to much of anything or anybody. They didn't know what the word *authority* meant.

A good, strict solid education was what Rachel had been used to in the Deep South. No longer did she hear the *whack* of wooden rulers smacking down on the knuckles of an unruly student. No more humiliation of putting your nose in a circle the teacher had drawn on the chalkboard because you were behaving badly. Harsh discipline at school was the norm in Alabama.

Once she got used to the strange and chaotic ways of the new classroom, she grew to like it. No more having to say *"Yes ma'am,"* or *"No ma'am,"* every time she responded to her teachers.

It was ironic that although having gone through such an abusive southern educational system as a child, Rachel never wavered from wanting to be a teacher herself when she grew up. Teaching was her passion. As a young child, she would line up all her dolls in a row and tirelessly teach them the Golden Rule for hours.

Now at twenty-eight, Rachel was a sixth-grade teacher at Redvine Elementary. For the most part, she loved all the kids. However, there was one exception, a boy named Billy Cooper. He was the class bully—as mean as a razor blade and as stubborn as a two-year-old not wanting to get off the swing. Rachel had been cursed by having him in her class for two years in a row now. However, whacking Billy across the knuckles with a ruler or making him stand in front of the class with his nose in a circle drawn on the chalkboard was not an option.

It took quite some time, years actually, but Rachel learned to love Seattle for what it was. She learned to see the mountains through the gray mist and the trees through the rain. In fact, there was a distinct beauty in the northwest's foliage—and it was always green. The Cascade Range, although it was the reason the rain stayed socked in on the west coast, was beautiful and had great ski resorts.

The Olympic Mountains were even more awesome and picturesque with their distinct jagged peaks that cut through the sky. But the one mountain that was paramount to all others was the majestic, breathtaking Mount Rainer, which stood at fifteen thousand feet and remained snowcapped all year round. Purple and pink hues would emanate from it at dawn and dusk on warm, clear summer days. Rachel hadn't yet climbed Mount Rainer, but it was one thing on her list of things she wanted to experience in the Great Northwest. The Seattle area was also surrounded by numerous lakes that were summertime playgrounds filled with kayaks, canoes, and jet skis.

Above all, what she yearned for most was the pure serenity and peace Seattle finally brought to her. If it was the ocean she wanted to see, she could just hop in her car, drive southwest, and in a few short hours would be walking barefoot on the beach—reveling in the crashing of the waves. She marveled at how each wave was so passionate, seemingly having a mind of its own and a unique story to tell.

At night, downtown Seattle would be buzzing with all walks of life, enjoying a myriad of unique bars and cuisine. Sometimes Rachel would join friends and venture out into the madness of people blowing off steam from their stressful workweek. She finally decided that the people weren't as odd as she once had thought. They just weren't as trusting, making it a little harder to get to know them.

Rachel, though plain and gangly as a child, had blossomed into a stunning beauty. Although all of her features were pretty, it was her eyes that captivated most people—not only with their extremely rare pale blue color, but with the warmth they would exude to anyone who looked into them. Her hair was long, straight, and blonde. It wasn't as thick as she would've liked, but because it was fine, it was extremely soft and had a glorious shine to it. She grew to be five feet seven—mostly legs—with an athletic build. Although she never wore braces, she had beautiful teeth and a magnificent smile.

Because of her looks and her heartwarming personality, getting any man she wanted was never a problem. But she was unable to hold on to the one man she had envisioned spending the rest of her life with. Jack Allen was what most women would describe as beautiful, in a masculine sort of way. His six-feet-two frame was lean and muscular. He had a face of model caliber with Caribbean-colored eyes, luscious lips, and sandy brown tousled hair. After two years of dating, they had become engaged.

Their relationship had been on the rocks for a while before they broke off the engagement, but the dreams Rachel had been having were the last straw for Jack. She didn't blame him for breaking up with her—not really. She often wondered if she wouldn't have done the same thing had the tables been turned.

Unfortunately, their demise was the result of her dreams. Anytime she tried to talk to him about them, he would roll his eyes and sarcastically dismiss it, shutting her down immediately. *"Predict the future,"* he would smirk. *"Isn't that a bit over the top?"* After enough conversation about her "predictions," he decided to move on. He figured it was time to get away from what he now considered to be his nutcase of a girlfriend whom he had once loved.

It didn't take long after their breakup for Jack to find another woman—considering his looks, women swarmed to him like bees to honey. Everything Jack wanted in a woman was something that Jessica Tallman was not. She was a frumpy, short, overweight brunette—devoid of any facial feature that would cause any normal man to waste a double take on.

Rachel knew exactly what had lured Jack to Jessica. It was one of the traits Jack had that never did sit well with Rachel—his love for money. The Tallman family had a majority share of Tallman Pharmaceuticals, a huge, profitable, and flourishing company. It was blatantly obvious to Rachel that Jack's decision to pursue Jessica had nothing to do with her as a person and had everything to do with her as a trust fund baby. Jessica was worth millions and Jack had ensnared her with his boyish charm. *Poor girl*, Rachel thought. Jessica was oblivious to Jack's ulterior motives—motives that had nothing to do with love.

To Rachel, his plan was quite transparent. One, Jack proposes to Jessica. Two, Jessica accepts with childlike giddiness. Three, Jack convinces her that there is no reason for a prenuptial agreement. Four, they get married. Five, Jack says bye-bye, taking half her assets with him.

Thinking back, Rachel could now see how manipulative Jack had been with her. He was a sly master, as smooth as butter. He could get her to do or not do just about anything. Love was truly blind. She'd asked herself many times why she had fallen in love with him—and worse yet, why did she still love him?

Rachel's parents, Anita and Carl Carter, had adopted her when she was just a few days old. They had tried for years to have a baby of their own and had gone through several rounds of in vitro fertilization. It was a sad irony that the one thing Anita wanted most in life was the one thing she was deprived of—a baby of her own.

"A baby is a baby," Carl told her irritably one day. "Stop fighting it, Anita. We have tried for years, and now it's time to look into adoption. It doesn't matter if it's biological or adopted! The baby will still be ours."

Finally, Anita agreed.

Rachel's birth mother was a sixteen-year-old runaway who lived on the streets, spent most of her life abusing drugs and alcohol, and sold her body for money. The young girl had obviously made some huge mistakes and bad choices in her life. Unfortunately, she was another throwaway kid who was on the eternal road to nowhere.

The one thing that Rachel's birth mother did do right, however, was to put Rachel up for adoption. Anita and Carl felt so fortunate that at least the young mother knew she would never be able to provide a good life for her baby. *Every once in a while, the dark side of humanity could provide something good,* Anita had thought to herself—a precious little bundle of a baby girl to call her own.

They vowed to themselves that they would raise Rachel in a calm and loving environment, which they did. They also vowed to each other that she was not to be spoiled. They agreed that spoiling their daughter rotten would only make for a difficult life later.

As a child, one thing Rachel wanted more than anything in the whole world was a horse. She pleaded to her parents for years to buy her one, but to her dismay, the closest thing she ever got to owning a horse was her large equestrian statue collection. As an adult, Rachel thought about buying herself a horse but decided against it once she realized how much money and time was needed to care for the beasts. As for pets, she settled on cats.

At fifty-six years old, Rachel's mother could be described as a carbon copy of the television version of Mrs. Santa Claus. She had bright blue eyes, surrounded by round wireframe glasses and snow white hair that she wore up in a bun most of the time. The wrinkles etched into her round jolly face confirmed her age, but her personality and energy kept her young. Her passion was cooking and raising kids. Despite any misfortunes that she was faced with, she always remained positive.

Anita's weight was a problem, and it was nobody's fault but her own. She was a gourmet cook and had decided a long time ago that she would always enjoy the pleasure of eating her own creations. Her doctor had once tried to convince her to drop some weight for her own health. She retorted back that she would rather sleep on a bed of nails than suffer through an exercise and diet program that would only make her miserable. She lectured back that it was the quality, not the quantity, of life that mattered, and that was that. Her doctor never brought the subject up again.

Chapter 3

Rachel woke up to what sounded like a thousand little fingers tapping on a computer keyboard. Having heard that sound a million times before, she knew immediately that it was Seattle's default weather—rain. In this case, because it was so cold, it was freezing rain. The phone suddenly rang and made her jump. Scolding herself for not turning the volume of the ringer down like she had meant to, she reached for the receiver with a blind hand.

"Hello?" she answered hoarsely.

"Oh no, did I wake you?" her mother's voice chirped in her ear.

"That's OK, Mom, I needed to get up anyway," she replied, a bit perturbed that she would call so early on a weekend. Rachel never could morph into a perky and chipper person in the morning. Those adjectives were saved for her mother. She loved her mother dearly, but early birds irritated her.

"I should say so. It's already ten o'clock. Did you sleep well?" her mother's singsong voice rang in her ear.

Rachel pushed her hair from her eyes, realizing she was in dire need of a haircut. She wasn't in the mood for a long drawn-out conversation this early, especially after the nightmare she'd had in the wee hours of the morning.

"Yeah, it was OK," she lied, stretching her body.

"You OK, honey? You don't sound well," Anita asked. She was a chain worrier about her daughter, and if she didn't have something to worry about, she would worry about not having something to worry about.

"Mom, I'm fine I'm just tired," Rachel said, clearing her throat, deciding not tell her mother about the nightmare. Telling her mother that she had just dreamed about a maniacal lunatic butchering her in a forest would just prompt worrisome questions from her mother, and she didn't want to relive the horror again. It was bad enough having dreamt it every night for the past two weeks.

Cali, her five-year-old calico cat, stretched her body and yawned as wide as an alligator. The cat made her slow trek up to Rachel and nuzzled as close to her face as possible, as if she wanted to be part of the conversation. On the purring Richter scale, she was off the charts. Because of Cali's interruption, it was hard to hear her mother, and Rachel could barely make out the question.

"Are you sure you're not getting sick? You don't sound like your normal self," her mother's voice wavered with concern.

"No, Mom, don't worry. I've just had a very hectic week at work," Rachel lied.

Again.

She rapidly changed the subject before her mother could ask her any more questions. "How are you doing, Mom? Did you get the foster child yesterday?"

"Not yet," Anita responded tentatively.

Her parents had been waiting for the foster child for weeks now, and the wait was wearing heavy on her mother.

"Not yet? Why not?"

"Honey . . . there's a bit of a problem," Anita said, ending with a long drawn-out sigh, which was unusual for her.

Her mother loved children, and once Rachel set out on her own, the loneliness and detachment drove her mother into a severe case of the empty nest syndrome. It was crystal clear to everyone that Anita's purpose in life was to nurture and love children. Without the scuffle of an active child running around the house, she was truly lost.

"Mom, for god sakes, what's up?" Rachel asked surprised.

"Well . . . there are two of them," she said anxiously.

"Two!" Rachel screeched.

"I know, I know, but it ends up that it's a set of twin boys and we don't think we should just take one," Anita replied sheepishly. "They really don't want to split the boys up, and we don't feel it's our place to separate them. I don't think I could live with that—especially since they're five years old." Her mother's guilt surged. "But I don't know if taking them both is a good idea either."

Even as energetic and devoted as her mother was with children, the challenge she was about to take on was a monumental one. *But taking only one of the boys certainly wouldn't be right*, Rachel realized. That wouldn't be fair to the kids, especially since they were twins.

"Mother, that's not even a choice. If you decide to get one, then you must take the other one! They belong together. They're identical twins. Splitting them up would be like spitting in Mother Nature's face. You can't do that to them," Rachel said, realizing after she spoke that she may have come across a little harsh.

Anita winced at the reprimand, but agreed. "I know. Taking them both is what I think we've decided to do."

Doubt began to swim in Rachel's mind. Two young boys would be a huge responsibility, but she didn't want to discourage her mother. "All I have to say—and I can say this because of my own experience—is that if anyone on this planet can take on something like this, it would be no one other than you and Dad. You do the parent thing really well, and I should know. I am sure they will love living with you guys."

"You have just got to see these boys! Two little toe heads with such sweet faces." Anita gushed. "If we take them, we can get them before Thanksgiving."

"I can't wait," Rachel replied, envisioning two little terrors running through the house at full speed. It would be chaos, but her mom thrived on happy chaos. Anita's heart would dance with pleasure when she was smack-dab in the middle of it all.

"Tell me about them?" Rachel asked curiously.

"My gosh, dear." Anita gushed even more. "They are such darling little boys. Their names are Austin and Preston. The social worker told me they were fraternal twins, but one look at their little faces and even I know that's not true. I know I don't have the best vision, but if these two are not identical, then I definitely need new glasses and a new brain to boot." She laughed. "We can't see one smidge of difference between the two. The only way we can tell them apart is that Austin has a cowlick on the left side, and Preston has one on the right."

Anita's voice cracked a bit. "Apparently, the birth mother lives on the streets and has been struggling to raise them. Terrible neglect . . . just terrible. There is one good thing though. I think the reason they have done as well as they have is because they have each other." A pang of guilt washed over Anita.

"I guess that means you get twice the joy and twice the trouble. It will be hard for you to determine which one to scold when they get into trouble, unless you get a good look at their cowlicks," Rachel laughed. "Mom," she added. "You and Dad are going to do just fine with those boys—they are going to love both of you."

"What do you have planned today?" Anita asked, changing the subject.

"I'm meeting Heather for breakfast this morning," she said, looking at the clock, shocked at how late it was. "In fact, I gotta go get ready, Mom. I'm going to be late."

"OK, dear. You tell Heather *hello* for me. Love you."

"Love you too, Mom."

Once Rachel hung up the phone, Cali lapped her face with her infamous sandpaper kiss, bringing her back to reality. "Hey, tuna breath, Mama needs some caffeine." The cat commented with a squeaky meow.

"What a good life you have, Cali. All you have to worry about is when your next meal will be and how many hours you can sleep today. Oh, and let's not forget that you don't even have to clean up after yourself." Cali gave her a few more kisses as if she understood her dilemma.

Her other cat, Dracula—named because his top incisor teeth stuck out when his mouth was closed—just stared at her from the bottom of the bed. "Hey, Drac." He didn't dare move. Cali would not have allowed his company. She was very territorial and despised the fact that he even breathed the same air. Drac joined the family a few years ago, and although he was a male and twice Cali's size, her hisses and bats always scared him enough to retreat to safer ground.

Cali had an attitude like most calico cats, and Dracula knew not to mess with it. Occasionally, Cali would allow him to sleep on the bed, but only at the opposite end and never closer to Rachel than she was. In Cali's mind, there was no such thing as an alpha male.

Rachel got out of bed and headed for the kitchen with Cali in tow—Dracula stayed behind on the bed until the coast was clear.

She grabbed the coffee grinder and dumped some coffee beans into it. She used to go to the little coffee hut down the street for her morning coffee, but her mother bought her a latte machine last Christmas, and she loved it for two reasons. One, she didn't have to get out of her pajamas to get her caffeine fix; and two, it saved her money—which she didn't have a lot of.

"OK, Cal, plug your ears," she warned the cat.

After she had made the perfect latte, she took one sip and relished the taste of the strong caffeine. Cali started squawking at full volume, protesting that she needed to be fed immediately. Rachel filled the kitty bowls with food and Cali began her usual inhalation. She took another sip of the coffee and walked down the hall and opened the front door.

"What do we have here today?" she murmured, reaching down to pick up the damp newspaper. God bless the paper boy for stuffing the bundle into a plastic bag on wet or snowy days, but it was a sorry effort because it got soaked anyway.

As usual, the damp paper carried the familiar nauseating stench of a wet dog—a relationship between the two eternally unknown to her. She really had never liked dogs and especially didn't like the way they smelled after they were in the rain. She brought the paper in and tossed it toward the table. Falling short, it ricocheted off the edge and landed on Cali's head. Without as much as a flinch, Cali continued to eat.

Dracula watched the incident from afar then looked up at Rachel with his huge green eyes and bucked fangs, and gave her his *"good-job-Mom"* expression. He had his own dish of food, but he was waiting for Cali to finish eating, lest he become the victim of a scorned feline. He had learned that the hard way when he once tried to approach his bowl when she hadn't finished eating out of hers. She had hissed at him, curling back her genetically coded spotty calico lips. Finally, she decided she was full, which wasn't very often considering her beach ball figure—another thing Cali didn't have to worry about.

Once in the clear, Dracula trotted over. "Best not to provoke the queen, huh?" Rachel addressed him. Dracula looked up at her and gave her his *"Cali-is-such-a-bitch"* expression.

Chapter 4

The first time Rachel saw Heather was when she plopped down in the chair in front of her in fifth grade. The most noticeable thing about her, Rachel decided, was her hair. It was a dark red color with corkscrew ringlets that bounced with every move she made. Sometimes she would put her curls in pigtails with different colored bows, and other days she would just let them run wild with nothing to rein them in.

The friendship between the two began when Heather turned around one day to ask if Rachel had an extra eraser. Heather was terribly shy and hadn't really wanted to turn around and ask, but she was desperate. All the erasers on her pencils had been chiseled down to mere nubs because she was such a nervous little girl. From the first time their eyes locked, they somehow knew they would be best friends forever.

Heather had huge hazel eyes with golden specks in them that reminded Rachel of the glitter she had used to decorate her Christmas stocking. The eyes were outlined with long auburn-colored lashes. She had a little turned-up nose with freckles that were splashed randomly across her face. Heather's mouth was small, pouty, and as red as a summer rose in full bloom. Her teeth were crooked, but Rachel surmised obviously not crooked enough for her parents to spring for the expense of braces. Heather's face, with all her features combined, created an image that by most people's standards wouldn't be labeled as pretty—but no one could ever deny that Heather's face was unique.

Heather's family had been quite poor and when they were kids Rachel always ended up sharing her lunch because Heather never seemed to have enough to eat in her old, rusty Barbie Doll lunch box. Heather's clothes were old and tattered, and she didn't have many. She wore the same dress almost every day to school. One day, at recess, the hem came undone. Heather's mother never took the time to sew it back up, so Rachel and Heather schemed to solve the problem with Scotch tape from their teacher's desk. But after one recess, the hem was hanging down again. Still, Heather wore it a million more times, just happy that she had a dress.

On Christmas day one year, Rachel called Heather to tell her about all the brand new gifts she had received. She wanted to rip her own tongue out when Heather responded that she had only received one gift—a hand-me-down doll that apparently belonged to a distant cousin who decided its next home would be the trash bin before it got intercepted by Heather's mom.

Rachel was shocked at the excitement she heard in Heather's voice, even though it was her only gift. Sure, the hair on the doll had been carelessly cut by her cousin and one of its legs kept falling off, but to Heather, it was the most precious thing in the world. It was the one thing she could call all her own.

Once they entered high school, the hell for Heather began. She became the target for bullying. Her attire was well below what the popular crowd considered "cool." Heather's clothes had obviously once hung next to the other rejects in a secondhand store. Her shoes had holes in the soles and had scuff marks everywhere. Heather had used her father's old crusty shoe polish one time in an attempt to make them look new—or newer. The kit didn't have the exact color she needed, so she used one that most resembled it. Unfortunately, it only made the shoes look worse by permanently altering the original color to a dingy shade of brown.

Rachel was a loyal friend to Heather and never left her side, but she never defended her either. Doing so would most likely catapult her into the net that held all the human targets chosen to bully. She loved Heather, but it wasn't worth the risk of getting the same treatment. Her friendship with Heather had already excluded her from the "in" crowd. *That counted for something, right?*

Because of the lack of funds for Heather to attend college, she started working right after she graduated high school. She landed a job with a well-known plastic surgeon named Kenneth Bankston. She started out as the receptionist but quickly advanced to his medical assistant—partially on merit, and unknown to Heather, more so on the doctor's admiration of her. He was enamored with this cute little redhead that had developed so much confidence over the past several months working for him. As her shyness subsided, she grew to love her job, and Dr. Bankston grew to love her.

After three years working for him, she became Mrs. Heather Bankston and entered into a lifestyle that couldn't be more opposite from what her childhood had been. Kenneth worshiped her and treated her like a princess, showering her with gifts and a quality of life that most women only dream of. They lived in a gorgeous and spacious home and she didn't have to work—although she did help out at the clinic when they were short staffed.

There was no limit to her shopping budget to stifle her desires. Manicures, pedicures, and massages once a week were the norm for her. Every once in a while, a pang of jealousy would rise up within Rachel, but it would quickly vanish. Heather had suffered a poor, atrocious childhood, and she deserved a good adulthood more than anyone else she knew.

Kenneth Bankston had one of the best reputations in the industry. Shortly after he and Heather were married, he expanded to three satellite clinics, all of which were profitable. Their business thrived beyond expectations.

At Rachel and Heather's ten-year high school reunion, Heather got her sweet revenge on those who had made her life so difficult, and Rachel finally got her chance to defend her. Heather drove her new convertible Mercedes into a parking slot right next to many of the girls who had taunted her. They were standing in a circle—some smoking cigarettes, some as big as heifers, and others looking quite matronly. The look on the girls' faces was priceless—jaws dropped one after the next.

"Reel your jaws back in, ladies," Rachel snickered. "Nice car, huh? This is *nothing* compared to the house she shares with her husband. I'm sure you all have heard of him—Dr. Bankston? The plastic surgeon? You've probably seen some of his ads on television or on billboards—*very successful.*"

Heather, embarrassed, charged on up the stairs, still intimidated by the girls. But she was glad that her best friend had the guts to do all the dirty work for her.

"Doesn't anyone have anything to say?" Rachel asked the circle of speechless women. She gave them one last dirty look, added a wink, and said, "Karma's a bitch, ladies."

Rachel and Heather met at Joe's Diner every Saturday morning, a tradition they had started in high school. Over the years, the walls of the diner had soaked up some of their deepest secrets, their tears, and their laughter. The tiny restaurant sat back off the road between a car dealership and a Dairy Queen. Walking through the door was like being thrown back into the 1950s. Black-and-white pictures littered the walls—women dancing in pedal pushers and saddle shoes, some with cat eye glasses, and men doing their best to look cool with their slicked-back ducktail hairstyles and cigarette-holding T-shirts. Hanging from the ceiling were two old-fashioned bicycles with wire baskets and their ding bells attached.

Rachel was led back to her booth by a stick-thin hostess who looked to be about twelve years old, her hair sprung up in pigtails like she had just been jumping rope at recess. Patsy Cline's *"Crazy"* was playing in the background.

"Will this be OK?" the elflike waitress asked.

"This is fine," Rachel replied with a whisper of a smile. Five minutes later, Rachel spotted Heather come through the door. Heather's eyes lit up when their eyes locked. She skipped over, leaned down, and gave Rachel a big hug. "Hey, honey, how are you?" Heather asked.

"I'm good," Rachel replied. Heather had on a large winter white coat overtop a cute little pink workout outfit, and was wearing new shoes that looked as if they had been purchased that day (and probably had been). Although Heather had just come from the gym, she didn't have a drop of sweat on her. Her fire red hair was bound up in a scrunch, with each ringlet dancing to its own tune.

"Ooh . . . what is this?" Heather asked, reaching out to touch the diamond pendant Rachel wore around her neck.

"Oh, I was finally able to hang my ex," Rachel smiled, referring to the diamond engagement ring she had recently transformed into a necklace.

Heather laughed at the comment. "What a jerk Jack is, but at least the diamonds came in handy," she said, sliding into the booth, peering at the sparkling gem.

"How about you? How was Greece?" Rachel asked, excited to hear about Heather's recent trip.

"It was so great . . . absolutely beautiful," Heather responded, her eyes dancing with excitement. "If I could live there, I would. Guess what?"

"What? You have that naughty face, what did you do?"

Heather whispered, "I sunbathed topless!"

"No! You have got to be kidding!" Rachel replied in shock. "Modest little Heather went topless? Tell me. I want to hear every detail."

"It was no big deal at all . . . everyone does it there," she responded with a sphinx-like smile.

"So you were able to show off your new set of boobs, huh?" Rachel asked, looking down at her own not-so-ample chest.

Heather noticed the gesture. "Oh . . . stop it, you are beautiful the way you are. But like I told you before, if you ever want to get a—"

Just then, an obese waitress waddled up to their table, looking like a tired penguin. Her expression was that of intense irritation. She was squished into a 1950s style red-and-white pinstriped uniform that looked to be three sizes too small, exposing every bump and bulge the poor woman had.

"What can I get for you?" the waitress snapped at Rachel, smacking her gum between nicotine-stained teeth.

"Uh . . . I'll have the French toast and some coffee, please." The waitress scribbled down the order with such force, Rachel thought the pen might snap in half. Rachel tossed a look of disbelief to Heather at how rude the waitress was.

Scowling, the waitress turned to face Heather. "I'll have the same," Heather blurted out before the waitress even had a chance to open her mouth. Rachel and Heather both just stared at the woman while she wrote down the order. She had a tight frustrated mouth with bright red lipstick that looked like she'd smeared on in a dark room. Her teased dull brown hair looked as chaotic as a tumbleweed.

"Do you want anything else?" the waitress asked, fluttering her fake black eyelashes. Thick black eyeliner surrounded her blue beady eyes and looked like it had been put on in the same dark room as her lipstick. They created a raccoon look, and based on her attitude, a rabid one at that.

"Uh . . . no," they said in unison.

She jammed the order pad into her pocket and reached for the water pitcher with her short nubby fingers that looked like they belonged to someone who had worked on a farm all their life. She recklessly poured water into each of their glasses with a good portion of it splashing on the table. Her fingernails were polished with an ugly shade of burnt orange. *If that was her effort at looking feminine, she failed miserably*, Rachel thought.

Her face was as wrinkled as a prune, her eyebrows looked like they were drawn on with a black permanent marker, and the poor woman had a huge pointy nose that was far too big for her face. She gave the girls one more disgusted frown before she briskly turned and waddled away, her hips swinging like the pendulum of a clock.

"Wow, isn't she pleasant," Heather said sarcastically.

"Yeah, a real sweetheart," Rachel agreed.

"Did you see her nose? You could put a set of snow skis on that honker and you'd be good to go," Heather commented. Rachel just smiled.

"Look, I need your help," Rachel said, distressed.

"Sure, honey—what is it?" Heather responded with her huge, curious hazel eyes.

"Remember the dream I had about the plane crash last year—you know, the one that happened on Christmas Eve? The plane I was supposed to be on?"

"How could I forget—the dream that sent Jack running and the one that creeped us both out because after you dreamed it, it actually happened."

"That's the one," Rachel responded with a shudder.

"Yeah, we thought you were psychic or something."

"Right, but then we decided it was just a fluke because nothing else weird happened," Rachel said.

"Yeah . . . so did something else happen that you dreamt about?" Heather inquired.

"It hasn't happened yet, but listen to this," Rachel said, tears welling up in her eyes. "God, I'm so scared."

"What? You are as white as a ghost!" Heather said, reaching across the laminated white tabletop, gently taking Rachel's hand in hers. "What is it, honey?"

After Rachel was able to compose herself enough to speak fluently, she took a deep breath, "You know about that Heartbreak Killer guy?"

"Yeah, the deranged maniac who's slaughtering all those women and leaving hearts behind at the murder scene?" Heather said.

"Yes . . . well for the last two weeks, I've been having dreams about getting murdered by him. I am so worried that it's another premonition or something."

"Oh," Heather said sympathetically, patting Rachel's hand. "Rach, it's probably just a dream. That Heartbreak Killer story has been all over the news and you're probably just freaked out about it."

"I don't think so, the dreams are too vivid," Rachel responded gravely.

Heather picked up her coffee and took a loud gulp. "Are they just as vivid and real as the plane crash dream was?"

"Yes. That's what scares me. Normal dreams aren't this vivid, believe me. This dream is so real—so real. You'd believe them too if you were having them."

"Why didn't you tell me about this earlier?" Heather asked.

"How was I supposed to tell you? You've been in Greece for two weeks," Rachel replied, leaning back on the booth's shiny red vinyl cushion.

"I don't care if I was in Timbuktu. You should have gotten a hold of me. You poor thing, you've been suffering with this for two weeks and you didn't tell me?"

"Heather, I didn't want to bother you on your vacation. I didn't know what to do," Rachel said, resigned.

"C'mon, Rachel. This is a little bit more important to me than snorkeling along the coast of Greece, don't ya think?"

"I know, I know. I should have called, but I didn't. Please don't get on my case now," Rachel said, pouring creamer into her coffee.

"I won't, but you and I have always pledged to tell each other things that are bothering us—especially something like this!"

The conversation was interrupted by the waitress meandering over with their breakfast. Rachel was starving—her stomach rumbling like a rock tumbler at full speed.

"More coffee?" the waitress spat after she placed their plates down.

"Yes, please," Heather said, pushing her cup toward the waitress. Rachel slid her cup over as well. The grumpy woman carelessly splashed coffee into both cups, and without another word, turned and waddled away.

"Heather, what do I do? I mean, I can't just sit in my condo all day hoping that it's just a dream," Rachel said, staring into her glass of water as if it held all the answers.

"The fact is, is that it probably *is* just a dream, so don't panic. On the other hand, if they are causing you this much distress, we need to do something about it."

"Like what? What am I supposed to do?" Rachel asked.

"First, tell me about the dream," Heather said, anxiously stabbing at the French toast with her fork.

"It starts out the same way every time," Rachel began. "I'm suspended really high above this forest. It's almost as if I'm floating in a bubble or something, but I can't move my arms or legs. It's at night, but I can see this man with a knife chasing a woman." Rachel paused to take a sip of coffee.

"Wait a minute," Heather said, furrowing her eyebrows. "I thought you said the killer was chasing *you*."

"That's the thing. At first, I don't know the woman he is chasing is me because I'm too high up. It's kind of like I'm watching a horror flick or something. Anyway," Rachel continued scooting her French toast around on her plate. "After he catches up to this woman, I start floating down to them. When I'm right next to them, I still don't know the woman is me because he has her facedown on the ground. So I can't see her face. I'm watching this whole thing happen and I'm screaming at this guy to let the girl go, but he doesn't hear me or see me and I still can't move my arms or legs. It's like I'm a ghost or something.

"Then I see him cut her throat. Then he takes out the wooden heart and writes '*Forgive Me*' on it. After that, he raises her arms and cradles the heart in her hands. It's not until the killer leaves and I turn the body over that I realize it's me."

"Geez, that *is* like a horror flick," Heather said intently.

"The really weird thing is, is that I can read the killer's thoughts and I can *feel* what he feels. He really doesn't want to kill. He feels guilty about murdering—it's really strange," Rachel said, staring out the window up at the gunmetal gray sky. She was holding her coffee cup so tight, her knuckles were as alabaster as the snow outside.

"A killer who doesn't want to kill? That is weird," Heather said with eyes as big as dinner plates.

Rachel's chin started to quiver, and Heather knew she was on the verge of tears. "It's OK, Rachel, it's OK," Heather comforted, dropping her fork to reach for Rachel's hand again.

Rachel continued to stare out the window, her face crawling with emotion. "He kills me with this huge knife—slashes my throat and nearly cuts my head off, just like all those other poor women he's killed."

"Slow down, Rach. We don't know for sure that any of this has any merit," she said, patting Rachel's hand. "I mean, it is creepy. But still, it's just a dream, and we don't know—"

"Stop telling me it's just a bad dream!" Rachel raged. As soon as the words spilled from her mouth, she regretted it. Heather was taken aback by Rachel's harshness. Her expression was that of being hit in the face with a brick.

"I'm sorry, I'm sorry. I didn't mean to yell at you, but believe me when I say it is more than just a dream—it is much more than that," Rachel said, tracing her pointer finger around the rim of her coffee cup.

"So you *really* think it's going to happen then?" Heather asked cautiously.

"I know if they don't find this madman first, then yes, I think it will happen," Rachel said, looking at Heather with haunted eyes. "I haven't told anyone. I don't want people, including you, to think I'm crazy or just making up a story for attention. I mean, hell—maybe I am crazy."

"Rachel Jo Carter!" Heather scolded. "First of all, I know you wouldn't lie about this. And secondly, you are not crazy! You shouldn't care what other people think anyway—especially me!"

"I'm sorry, I'm just scared," Rachel said, shrinking back into the comfort of the booth cushion.

"I can see why you're terrified, Rachel. It does seem odd. Maybe you are psychic after all. I mean, you've always been intuitive, even before the plane crash," Heather commented. "So now we just have to find a way to prevent this from happening."

"I agree, but the question is, what can I do?" Rachel's face was painted with panic. "I don't want to brush this off and end up dead."

"I know," Heather responded. "Don't worry, we will figure out a solution. No one is going to take my best friend away from me." Rachel could see Heather's mind start to tick like a clock—something she always did when faced with a dilemma. Finally, Heather's eyes lit up like she just had a miraculous epiphany.

"I have an idea," she said, reaching for her gigantic flamingo-colored purse sitting beside her on the seat. Frantically, she started rummaging through it—her arms going deeper and deeper. Heather started pulling things out of her purse and throwing them onto the table—her wallet, pens, makeup, a calculator, a water bottle, an entire bottle of contact lens solution, a book, wrinkled-up receipts, and other things Rachel couldn't even imagine putting into her own purse.

Considering how long it was taking Heather to find whatever it was she was looking for, Rachel decided the purse was a flamingo-colored black hole.

While Rachel waited, she overheard a conversation going on between two women in the booth next to them. An enraged woman was ranting and raving to her friend about what a deadbeat dad her ex-husband was; that she was thoroughly pissed off about having to support her kids without a penny's worth of child support from the bastard. The last thing Rachel heard before tuning back into Heather's frantic rummaging was that the woman was seriously thinking about purchasing a shotgun.

"I want you to see someone," Heather said, continuing to dig.

"Finally!" she said, pulling out her pink cell phone.

Rachel's eyes grew narrow. "It better not be the police because I refuse to go there. They would think I was a joke and laugh me out of the station."

Heather didn't respond. Instead, she flipped through the contact list on her phone until she found who she was looking for. She pressed the phone securely between her ear and shoulder.

"I mean it, Heather," Rachel warned. "Don't call the police!"

Heather sighed and rolled her eyes in response to Rachel's panic. "I'm not calling the police."

Rachel sighed with relief. "Good. You know, if I were to go to the police, they really would just throw me out of the station."

Half a second later, Rachel's panic started to rise again. "Then who *are* you calling?"

"I'm calling a friend who I work out with at the gym," Heather replied.

"Why? I don't want to tell anyone about this," she said frostily, scrunching her napkin into a little ball—a nervous habit she had always had. "I don't want anyone other than you to know about this. I only told you because you are my best friend and I trust you implicitly." Rachel threw the wadded-up napkin aggressively across the table, where it landed just shy of the condiments.

"Well then, why don't you trust me now?" Heather shot back. The comment caught Rachel off guard, leaving her speechless.

The silence between them made it easy for Rachel to hear the ringing emanating from Heather's phone. "What makes you think that whoever you are calling will even believe this? I don't have any evidence."

"You don't need evidence, Rachel," Heather said, looking up at her. "We are not dealing with the police. What you need is an experienced psychic."

Rachel narrowed her eyes. "A psychic?"

"Yes," Heather confirmed. A second later, she held up her pointer finger to signal to Rachel that the person on the other end of the line had picked up.

"Hey, Claudia, how are you?" Heather asked while pouring more syrup onto her French toast with her free hand. Rachel heard a woman responding through the phone and the two talked for a few seconds regarding their workout routine. Finally, Heather said, "Hey, I need a favor from you. Do you still have the number to that psychic you used to go to?"

Rachel heard Claudia squawk something. She pulled another napkin out of the dispenser and started wadding. Heather also pulled a napkin out, groped for one of the fifty pens that were sprawled out on the table, and scribbled a name and a phone number on it.

"Thanks, Claudia, see you at the gym tomorrow." She quickly snapped the phone shut, threw it into her purse, and slid everything that was occupying half the table back into her flamingo-colored black hole with no organization whatsoever.

"Heather, this is crazy," Rachel said, frustrated.

"Rachel, this person is not some fly-by-night psychic trying to make a few bucks by giving empty promises. Claudia says this woman is highly credible and incredibly accurate. Apparently, the police use her on cases when they are searching for missing people or tracking down murderers. Better yet, apparently, this person specializes in dreams. She's so prominently known that she's even been a guest on national television and radio talk shows. And she's written several best-selling books," Heather spilled persuasively.

"I don't know, Heather, I don't like this kind of stuff," Rachel replied, unconvinced.

"Well, if anyone can explain this type of thing, it would be her. And who better than a psychic to know if someone else is psychic? Besides, what could it hurt? Here," she said, sliding the napkin across the table to Rachel.

Rachel hesitantly picked up the napkin and looked at Heather skeptically.

"Call her!"

"All right, I'll call her."

"You are *going* to call her, no backing out."

"I will—I promise."

"Good." Heather smiled through her beautiful veneers.

Chapter 5

Rachel's hand rested on the telephone receiver for several seconds before she quickly pulled it back. What was she thinking? She had never been to a psychic before. In a way, it seemed ridiculous to call this Monica Rupert lady; but in another way, she wouldn't care if Monica was Winnie the Pooh as long as she had the answers.

But then again, did Rachel really want to know her future? What if she was told that the dream was accurate and she was going to die? Did she really want to hear that she would be sliced up by some crazy man? The thought of not calling Monica flitted through her mind, but the wrath of Heather coming down on her with a sledgehammer prompted her to pick up the phone and dial.

After three rings, the answering machine clicked on. *Thank God,* Rachel thought. She was so nervous about talking to Monica live. Surprisingly, Monica's greeting sounded normal. *"Hello, this is Monica Rupert. I am currently with a client or out of the office, please leave a message and I will be sure to call you back as soon as I can."* Beep . . .

"Oh, hi, uh . . . my name is Rachel, Rachel Carter," she said hesitantly. "You were recommended to me and I would like to set an appointment up with you." Rachel left her number and quickly attempted to put the receiver back on the cradle, but her hands were trembling so bad, she missed and it bounced on the counter. Grabbing the receiver again, she succeeded on her second try. *Good. Done. No sledgehammer this time.*

That afternoon, the phone rang and a surge of dread raced through Rachel's body. "Hello," she said tentatively after she put the receiver to her ear.

"Hello, is this Rachel?" For a split second, Rachel thought of hanging up, but then thought of the sledgehammer again.

"Yes, this is she."

"Hello, Rachel. This is Monica Rupert, returning your phone call. How can I help you, dear?" She sounded normal enough. Rachel had expected something quite different—maybe a woman with a voice as rough as jagged wood.

"Well . . . uh . . . my friend suggested I give you a call. I would like to come in and see you." Rachel heard her heart pounding in her chest like a drum and a heat wave darted through her.

"We can certainly do that," Monica's voice sparked up. "When would you like to come in?"

"Sometime this week, if possible," Rachel blurted out and then took another deep breath. "I'm a schoolteacher, so I would need to book a late afternoon appointment."

"Let's see," Monica responded. Rachel heard fingers tapping away on a computer. "Would next Thursday at five work for you?"

Without even looking at her schedule book, Rachel told her that would be fine. "Thanks," Rachel quickly said and put the phone down without saying good-bye. *How rude was that?* She slid down into the kitchen chair and put her head in her hands.

"I did it, Drac, I did it," Rachel muttered. Dracula sat on the floor beneath her, purring—his huge green eyes looking at her sadly as if he understood her frazzled nerves.

Thursday afternoon came a little too quickly for Rachel. She had no idea how this meeting would turn out, and she was absolutely terrified. A car behind her honked, startling her back into reality. She looked up and the light was green. How long had she been sitting there? Had she gone through any red lights? She had no idea. Thoughts were screaming through her mind, yet it was as if a thick fog prevented her from making any sense out of them.

As soon as she cleared the intersection, the irritated driver behind her honked again, accelerated at mach-five speed, and recklessly passed her. The driver showed Rachel his gratitude by flipping his middle finger at her. "Whatever," Rachel uttered under her breath. "If you only knew, flipping me off is the least of my worries."

"Arriving at destination on right," the monotone voice of the GPS squawked. Rachel slowly pulled up to the curb, stopped her car, and examined the house. *This can't be it,* she thought—it certainly didn't look like a place of business. She expected the place to be located in one of those run-down strip malls in a seedy part of town, where addicts hung out and bums filled the streets. And where was the "Palm Reading" neon sign?

She checked the address on the crinkled-up napkin Heather had given her. Unless Heather had written it down wrong—which was entirely possible, considering her best friend could be quite ditzy at times—she was at the right place.

"Here we are, Clunker," she said—a name she had given her fifteen-year-old car ever since the service bills started out weighing the value of the car. Every morning, she said three Hail Marys before twisting the key in the ignition, hoping it would start. When it did, she considered it a true blessing. The car was basically held together by Bondo glue and a prayer. She loved her job as a schoolteacher, but the pay sucked. Her measly salary could barely pay the bills as it was—getting another car was simply out of the question. Ironically, educating the next generation's presidents and successful business entrepreneurs hung low on the professional pay scale.

The wind had picked up, and when Rachel stepped out into the frigid air, her hair felt like tiny needles slapping her face. A ray of sun split the granite sky, transforming the snow on the ground into a beautiful array of crystals. Clunker's tired metal groaned as she slammed the door shut. Tentatively, she started her trek through the snow up to the house. Because of the ice and snow, she treaded lightly, not wanting to slip. She noticed that someone had taken enough care to sprinkle rock salt onto the driveway and walkway, so she hastened her pace, but not by much. She couldn't afford an injury, especially if she ended up having to run from a psycho killer.

In front of her sat a huge white country-style home with blue shutters and a blue door to match. She stepped up on to the front wraparound porch, focusing her eyes on the gold address numbers nailed into the wood by the front door, confirming she was at the right place.

Hanging from the porch ceiling was an old-fashioned double swing. A vision flashed through her mind of an old couple huddled together, holding hands—an anomaly of two people who had defied the odds of a society dominated by divorce and broken families. Wasn't "til death do us part" just a hollow vow newlyweds flapped their jaws to on their wedding day? True, her parents had weathered the marriage storm, but so many people she knew hadn't been so lucky.

There were blue-colored planter boxes that hung below each front window. They held nothing but cracked frozen dirt, but she envisioned them to be overflowing with petunias and tulips in the spring and summer, which would add a nice touch. Any plant or flower she had ever bought seemed to die within the first week, regardless of her mother's advice on how to keep them alive, so she finally stopped wasting her money. It was also useless to buy fresh flowers for the house. They looked beautiful, but the problem was Cali and Drac found them to be just as beautiful in an edible sort of way. If they did get a stomach full of the flowers, Rachel would no doubt see the result of their intestinal strife on the carpet.

Once Rachel determined she was at the right place, she rapped on the door using the big gold lion's head knocker. She was analyzing how fierce and mean it looked when she heard someone coming to the door. Rachel snapped back to her stoic stance, her heart racing. She had reached the point of no return. The only thing standing between her and knowing her future was that blue door. When Monica opened it, Rachel was surprised at what she saw. The woman standing before her offered up a warm and welcoming smile. "You must be Rachel," she said in a sweet, inviting voice.

"Yes," Rachel said. It was hard to estimate the woman's age because she had a mature face, yet her skin was like porcelain. She must have either been blessed with it or smart enough to stay away from the tanning salons that most Washingtonians flocked to. Since the state had so little sun, it was either spend time in a tanning bed or walk around transparent, especially those who were so-called *blessed* with fair skin.

Monica's hair was chestnut brown and cut extremely short—a style that looked great on her, but one that most women wouldn't be caught dead in. She had warm green eyes—the kind that looked at you as if they'd known you forever. Her tall thin frame was accentuated by the slate blue-colored suit she wore. Encircling her neck was a fuchsia-and-blue-colored scarf secured in front with a neatly tied knot. Attached to her lapel was a beautiful pin with alternating blue and pink stones. The woman was immaculate. If Rachel didn't know any better, she would have placed her as an attorney or a professor—certainly not a psychic.

"Come on in, dear," Monica said, motioning her into the house. Rachel followed her down a long hardwood-floored hall. Looking to her left, she saw an elegantly decorated living room, painted soft sage with white wainscoting. Two large green vintage couches faced each other, separated by an ornate antique coffee table. On top of the coffee table was a large glass-blown bowl perched on a wooden pedestal. It had always perplexed Rachel how such masterpieces could be created by blowing glass. A huge fireplace, surrounded by a large white mantle, was built into the back wall with a large painting that looked to be authentic and expensive hanging above it. The front window covering was a swag made out of plum-colored material.

Looking to the right, Rachel observed the dining room with walls painted the same color. The room also carried a vintage theme. There was an ornate mahogany table placed in the middle of the room. Above the table was an enormous chandelier that hung from a vaulted ceiling. Against one wall stood a matching china hutch filled with plates, saucers, and ceramic angels. Sitting in one corner of the room was an antique tea cart with intricate china cup and saucer sets placed on it. She noticed that both rooms had hardwood floors. Rachel had always wanted hardwood floors. Not just because they looked classy. She was allergic to cats—something she didn't find out until she had added Cali and Dracula to her family.

On the hallway walls were photos of a boy that appeared to be hung in chronological order: the boy as an infant, a toddler, and now as a young boy.

The clicking against the floor as Monica walked down the hall prompted Rachel to look down at the source of the sound. Monica's shoes were the same color as her suit. *What a class act she was,* Rachel thought. Her jitters were finally subsiding.

Monica opened a door at the end of the hall and invited Rachel into her office. Rachel's eyes scanned the room as she entered. Again, not what she expected. She didn't see a crystal ball or tarot cards or witchlike symbols—things that she would associate with a psychic's place of business. It didn't look any different than the office of any other credible professional.

"OK, dear," Monica chirped. "Sit down wherever you would like and make yourself comfortable." Rachel chose to sit down on a maroon-colored leather love seat. It felt like a huge marshmallow whose main agenda was to completely swallow her up.

"Can I get you some coffee? Tea? Water?" Monica asked.

"Uh, coffee sounds good," Rachel responded.

Monica walked toward the door. "Cream? Sugar?"

"Cream would be great . . . just a little," Rachel responded using her thumb and index finger to illustrate how much she wanted.

"OK . . . I will be right back," Monica said, her eyes sparkled like a million diamonds. "You just sit back and relax."

Rachel glazed her hand over the cushions of the love seat, and although it was leather, it felt like satin. This woman certainly didn't skimp on furniture. The taupe-colored walls were warm and welcoming. One of the walls wasn't actually a wall at all. It was a large window that looked out onto a creek. Although frozen now, she surmised the soft babbling sound would add a nice touch during warmer climates.

In front of her was a cherrywood coffee table with a beautiful dried flower arrangement placed in the middle of it. Beneath her lay a black-and-gray checkered rug that brought out the colors in the two paintings on the opposite wall. The paintings weren't of any particular object, but rather the kind that looked as if the artist had thrown paint onto the canvas from several feet away. Still, they somehow looked nice and tied in nicely with the decor.

The other wall was mainly taken up by a large cherrywood bookcase that held several books. They were of all different subjects—hypnosis, psychic powers, reading into the mind, dreams. The book that hit her as most ironic was the one labeled, "The Gift of Being Psychic." *A gift? More like a curse,* Rachel thought.

Rachel's eyes darted over to Monica's desk, also made of cherry. Too luring to resist, she struggled to her feet—the love seat not wanting to let her go. She made sure to keep her ears peeled for the clicking noise as she quietly padded over to Monica's desk.

On the desk were a few of the normal office paraphernalia—a blotter, a small wooden file rack, and one of those pen and pencil holders that must be for show because Rachel had never seen anyone actually use them.

Her eyes landed on a photo of Monica with what must've been her husband and the child whose portrait lined the hall. The man in the photo standing beside Monica was a portly man in an ill-fitted suit, who looked like he hadn't seen the inside of a gym in quite some time. *Interesting couple,* Rachel thought. *Sometimes opposites do attract.*

Standing in front of them was their son. He looked to be about five or six. Having the same facial features as Monica, there was no doubt as to who his mother was.

On the other side of the desk was a bouquet of pink roses that were arranged in a clear vase with pink dye swirled within the glass. There was a card entwined within the stems that read, "*Happy Anniversary, Sweetheart*" and was signed "*Bruce.*" Behind the desk was a matching credenza. Placed on top was an orange-and-blue large bowl that also looked to be glass blown.

When Rachel heard the clicking, she rushed and sat back down on the love seat, hoping it would sink all the way back down before Monica came in; otherwise, it would be obvious from the extraction of air that she had been up snooping around. Monica entered a mere millisecond after the couch had stopped hissing.

"Here you go, dear. Be careful, it is very, very hot . . . I just made it," Monica said, cautioning her like she would a small child being handed a hot bowl of macaroni and cheese. Rachel was astonished at how normal this woman was—pleasant, actually.

After gently handing her the coffee, Monica walked over and sat down in a leather maroon-colored wingback chair across from Rachel. "Nothing better than a nice hot cup of coffee on a cold crisp day," Monica said, smiling as she took a cautious sip.

"Almost as good as hot buttered rum on Christmas Eve." The words tumbled out of Rachel's mouth. *Where did that random thought come from?*

Monica smiled, hugging her mug in her hands, and crossed her long legs. More uncensored verbiage spilled out of Rachel's mouth before she could think. "You certainly don't look like what I had expected."

"Were you a little worried that I might greet you in my long flowing black dress and lure you back into my cosmic world—crystal ball and all?" Monica smiled teasingly.

Rachel forced a smiled in return. "I must admit, I didn't dare choose tea when you asked me what I wanted to drink. I didn't want you to read the leaves." She felt her face redden a bit. Monica threw back her head and laughed.

"Tell me how I can help you?" Monica asked, her mood changing into a more serious expression, like a scientist may look while examining a rare specimen of bug.

"Well," Rachel said, taking a sip of her coffee to buy time. "I've had a dream every night for the past two weeks about being murdered in some forest by the guy they're calling the Heartbreak Killer. Do you know who I'm talking about?"

"Yes, I've heard of him on the news," Monica responded.

"Anyway, he chases me down and kills me just like he does the other women—slits my throat, leaves the heart . . . the whole nine yards," Rachel said, focusing on the steam rising from her coffee mug. "Vivid . . . the dreams are so vivid." Not wanting to break Rachel's train of thought, Monica remained silent.

"At first I just thought it was a bad dream, you know," Rachel said, shrugging her shoulders. "But because the dreams are so vivid and because I've had them every night for the past two weeks, I think it may be something more, you know. Anyway, it's scaring the hell out of me and I want to know if it's some kind of premonition." She looked up at Monica. No flinch, no slight sarcastic smile, nothing except an expression of what seemed to be genuine concern.

"Have you ever had dreams that were this vivid before?" Monica asked. "More importantly, have you ever had a premonition before?"

Rachel gently placed her coffee cup on a ceramic coaster sitting on the end table next to her. It was decorated with green and purple grapes that looked to be hand painted. "Yes, last year, that plane crash that happened? The one in San Diego—you know, where everyone was killed?"

"Yes, that was tragic," Monica replied, nodding slowly.

"I dreamt about that—every detail—before it happened. What was eerie about that dream was that I was actually supposed to be on that plane. I would have died along with all of the rest. Have you ever heard of dreams actually being premonitions?"

Monica looked directly into Rachel's eyes. "Oh yes—you've come to the right place. I actually specialize in dream interpretation. Some dreams are meant to caution. Some dreams aren't—they are simply dreams."

Rachel crossed one leg over the other and started pumping it nervously. "Because of the plane crash premonition, I am wondering if I may be psychic myself. Something I really don't want to be. No offense, of course."

"None taken," Monica smiled. "It is entirely possible that you may be psychic."

"It's spooky though. I swear to God, Monica, I am not lying about this."

"I believe you," Monica said simply.

With that, Rachel said, "I should have said something to someone. All those people on that plane would be alive if I had just had the guts to warn someone. The guilt is unbearable at times."

"You can't blame yourself. No psychic trusts their instincts initially. I didn't trust mine. You can't blame yourself for what happened. At that time, you just thought it was a vivid dream. You did take precaution by cancelling your flight, but you had no idea the crash would actually happen," Monica consoled.

"You've got to let the guilt go. If you had tried to warn the passengers, they probably would have laughed at you and gotten on the plane anyway. People are going to do what they are going to do, regardless of any warnings they may get from you or anyone else. Let me start by telling you that you are not a nutcase or a freak or any other word some people refer to when things don't make sense to them," Monica assured. "Furthermore, it's important for you to know that we all have some degree of psychic abilities—everyone does."

Monica put her coffee cup down and leaned toward Rachel, lacing her long fingers together. "It's just that some people ignore it—they block it out, while others embrace it. Those people who do ignore their own intuitiveness are usually the ones who are scared of it or simply don't believe that anything outside the physicality of this world exists. They won't accept that strange things can and do happen to them that may not be just coincidence."

Monica reached for an analogy. "Like thinking about the phone ringing seconds before it does. In spite of popular belief, that's not just a coincidence. The more we accept our psychic abilities, the more we begin to trust them. Those who shut out this sense, if you will, would just think that the phone ringing is a random thing. It's too scary for them to think otherwise. They won't let their conscious mind believe what their psychic mind is trying to tell them. However, those who do allow their intuitiveness to talk to their conscious mind realize that their predictions may be valid. Psychics have allowed this additional sense, if you will, to come kicking and screaming through. Psychics *believe* that they're psychic mind can talk to their conscious mind and predictions and premonitions can be very real. They also know that they have absolutely no control over this phenomenon."

"Well, again, no offense, but I'm not really open to this psychic stuff. I truly don't want to believe in it. That's why it was hard for me to even call you. Even though I had the plane crash premonition, I kept telling myself it was just a fluke or something. I don't want to have this sense or recognize it—it scares me," Rachel said.

"That's my case and point, Rachel. I'm sorry dear, but it sounds as if you may be subject to this phenomenon. If so, you really have no choice but to accept it—unless you want to live with your head buried in the sand for the rest of your life." Monica's words clenched Rachel's heart like a vise.

Still, she was unconvinced, so Monica reached for another analogy. "Look at it this way . . . a short person cannot make themselves tall just because they hate being short. It's impossible. Unless they wear platform shoes, of course. Since you can't fight it, you may as well accept it and learn how to deal with it—only then will your torment ease up. I understand what you are feeling, Rachel—the fear and the frustration. Remember that I have the same gift that you have. But please, trust me when I say that your ability to cope with it will become easier once you come to accept it."

"I don't look at it as a gift," Rachel said. "It's more of a curse."

"Some people do think of it as a curse," Monica said. "I'm sure you've heard of those people who are surrounded by dead people and spirits all the time. Many of those people find it to be very distracting, terrifying, and sometimes annoying, but there is nothing they can do to separate themselves from it. It is part of who they are."

Monica stood up and asked Rachel if she wanted more coffee. Rachel looked like she was in a trance and handed Monica her coffee cup without even looking at her. Her brain tuned into Monica walking down the hall, causing her to snap back to her senses. Rachel's mind was spinning like a tea cup at a theme park as she tried to figure out how she was going to deal with her so-called psychic abilities. *Oh dear god, how am I supposed to handle all this? I don't want it—I just don't want it.*

She was startled when Monica came through the door, even though she was given fair warning by the clicking shoes on the hardwood floor. "Here you go, dear," Monica said, carefully handing her the mug. Monica sat back down and crossed her legs. "Now, let's talk about your dreams so I can determine whether they are premonitions or just nightmares. Tell me about the plane crash dream."

"OK, I will try. It's scary to even talk about that dream. I mean, it brings back all the fear and the emotions I experienced."

"It's OK, I'm right here and you will be just fine," Monica assured. "Remind yourself that you are not in the dream now, so you are safe."

After what seemed like an eternity, Rachel reluctantly began. "The dream starts out where I am just sitting in my seat on the plane, reading," she paused and took a deep breath. "Everything was fine for the majority of the flight, but then, all of a sudden, there was this loud explosion—like an engine blew out or something." Rachel closed her eyes—lines appeared on her face.

"Then the plane started vibrating and rocking back and forth—tipping from one side to the other. People were screaming and praying. I started to feel faint and I broke out in a sweat—my heart was racing. It was so surreal. I feared I was going to die. I saw everyone looking around with panicked faces. Babies were screaming out of control, scared just like the rest of us—God, those poor babies—their faces," Rachel said, putting her face in her hands. "They didn't even get a chance at life." Rachel opened her eyes and looked angrily into Monica's face. "Where the *hell* is the justice in that?" She closed her eyes again—her chin quivering.

"Keep going, Rachel, keep focused on the dream," Monica redirected her.

"All the stuff in the overhead bins was thrown out and hitting people. People were getting out of their seats—like that would somehow save them. I stayed in my seat, but I remember getting hit in the head by something falling—I don't know what it was, but I remember it hurting. To tell you the truth, I wish it had knocked me out so I didn't have to experience the plane falling. People were being thrown around the cabin, slamming into things and into each other," she said, nervously twirling the opal ring on her finger that Jack had given her—something she was still unable to part with.

"And then the plane flipped over and went vertical. That's when I knew, everyone knew, they would be dead in less than a minute." Rachel opened her eyes and stared straight ahead—her face frozen—no expression. "I can't even describe the fear I felt as the plane was dropping down. It was the most horrible feeling. Thank God I didn't feel the impact when the plane nosedived into the ocean—it happened so fast. Then the next thing I know, I'm floating above everything—almost as if my soul had left my body. I saw all the plane parts floating in the ocean. I saw the bodies, even my own. I saw suit cases, papers, airplane seats—some with people still in them . . ." Rachel buried her head in her hands again.

"I knew at that point that everyone was dead—and I died right along with them. I guess I know what it feels like to die now. But . . . ," Rachel said, her words trailing off. She looked up at Monica with deep sadness migrating across her face. "I don't understand. I was supposed to be on that plane."

She sobbed, her shoulders shaking uncontrollably. "I should be dead. I mean, the only difference between me and all those poor people is that I didn't get on the plane. I made a choice not to get on that plane because of a dream. They made the wrong choice without even knowing it."

Monica picked up a box of tissues and walked them over to Rachel. "Well, the good thing is that you are here and very much alive," Monica said, focusing back on the matter.

"I know Monica, but why—why did I live?" Rachel asked, dabbing her eyes with the tissue

"Because it wasn't your time to die yet."

"I feel like I'm running from my own death and it's just a matter of time before it catches up to me." Rachel rationalized, "It's kind of like that movie—I think it was called *Final Destination*—you know the one where those kids were destined to die in a plane crash, but they somehow narrowly escape it. But just when they think they're safe, death comes and gets them after all."

"I don't think that's what is happening here. In this situation, it may have been that someone who has already passed away is trying to protect you. Or . . . maybe trying to send you a message—tell you something." Monica said.

Rachel looked confused. "Tell me something?"

"Yes, you see, these types of dreams can come from a variety of sources. They can come from our own psychic intuition, like we've been talking about, or they may be sent from someone on the other side."

Rachel shook her head with a smirk on her face. "Sorry, but I don't believe in ghosts. I mean, like I said before, I'm not even sure I believe in psychics," Rachel said. "And secondly, I don't have any loved ones on the other side yet that I know of, at least not anyone who would want to send a message to protect me. I certainly haven't done any life-altering favor for anyone who is now dead to merit a message from them on how to save my life. No—that makes no sense." Rachel took a breath and looked up to focus back on Monica.

"It may not be a person," Monica said.

Rachel's face went white. "What do you mean it may not be a person? Don't scare me—I don't need this to be anything scarier than it already is."

"If this dream is in fact a warning to you, then whatever or whoever is sending you the dreams—if that is even the case—is made of good energy. But let's not jump to conclusions before we even know what is happening. I can assure you that if it is an entity, it is a good one, OK?

One of protection," Monica consoled. "It may not make sense now, but it may later, after we dive deeper into it."

Rachel took a large swallow of her coffee, scalding her tongue in the process. "OK, but even if the dream I'm having now is a warning, I don't know how to avoid it. I don't know how, when, or where it may happen. I don't know where this forest is, it could be anywhere. I have no advance warning. At least in the crash dream, I had the flight number and knew to avoid it. There won't be any warning signs for this one. I can't just lock myself in my home all day and night to prevent my murder."

"That's why we have to do what we have to do next," Monica said, "And this is not going to be easy for you."

Rachel felt her throat constrict. "What are you going to ask me to do?"

"I'm going to join you in the murder dream."

All the blood drained from Rachel's face. "What? How are you going to do that?"

"I am going to what I call *connect* with you this time, and we will relive the dream together," Monica explained.

"How are you going to do that?" Rachel asked, confused.

"It's what I get paid for," Monica said, smiling.

Monica walked over and sat down on the couch next to Rachel and reached for her hands. "Now what you need to do this time is a little different. You need to close your eyes and focus on every detail of the dream. Try not to think of anything else. I will need to hold hands with you. Don't open your eyes and don't break from my hold, because if you do, I will lose the connection."

"Do I need to talk to you while I'm visualizing the dream, or should I stay quiet?" Rachel asked.

"Talk as much as you'd like. I will be able to see what happens when you visualize it, but sometimes it helps if you narrate it as we go."

"OK," Rachel said, closing her eyes. She wasn't sure exactly how to start, but she said the first thing that came to mind. "It starts out where I am floating high above a forest at night. Down below, I see a man chasing a woman. I don't know that the woman being chased is me at first because she's too far away."

"Good, Rachel, good, I can see it now. I'm there with you," Monica said.

Rachel was shocked by Monica's words and opened her eyes abruptly. "You are actually there with me?"

"Yes, Rachel, I *was* there, but now I am not. Please keep focused. Keep your eyes *closed*, visualize the dream, and keep a hold of my hands—that is the only way I will be able to connect with you and stay connected."

"Oh, OK, sorry," she said, closing her eyes again. "The man chasing her is getting closer and closer, do you see that?"

"Yes, he's wearing all black."

Rachel opened her eyes again, "I can't believe—"

Monica cut Rachel off instinctively, knowing she had opened her eyes. "Rachel, Rachel, you must keep your eyes closed, and focus only on the dream. When you open your eyes, I disconnect and I lose my vision," Monica explained. "It can then become very difficult to reconnect with you."

"Sorry . . . sorry . . . ," Rachel apologized again. She kept silent and visualized the dream again.

After several seconds, Monica said, "OK, I'm back in your dream again . . . go on. Focus on what you see."

Rachel's voice became stressed. "She's running, trying to get away from him and she doesn't see the tree root. She trips on it and falls. She can't get up at first."

"Yes, she's having a hard time getting up. It looks like it's her ankle? Maybe she twisted her ankle because now she's hobbling?"

"So you see that too?"

"Yes, I can see her struggling with her ankle just as you see it," Monica responded assuringly.

"I can read the killer's thoughts," Rachel said. "Can you?"

"Yes, I can read his thoughts as well. He has a tremendous amount of guilt and keeps repeating what a *kind* and *gentle* man he is." Rachel was in disbelief at this whole process but kept her eyes shut.

A few seconds or so passed in silence. "OK, now he's caught up to the woman . . . now he's grabbing her hair, and he's pulling her to the ground. He's too strong. She can't get away," Rachel cried, her voice shaking. "And . . . I can't help her."

"It's OK, Rachel, it's OK," Monica soothed. "There is nothing you can do. He's too strong. There was nothing you could have done."

Rachel let go of Monica's hands at that point and the connection was lost again. "I don't understand . . ."

"I lost connection, Rachel. Let's get back to the dream. You *must* close your eyes and do not open them. You also *must not* let go of my hands. When we are done with the connection, I promise you, I will explain everything and answer any questions you may have, OK?"

"OK," Rachel whispered. She closed her eyes again.

A minute or so passed. "Now I'm starting to descend from high above. It's like I'm floating. I can't move my arms or legs, but I'm able to float down to them," Rachel paused. "Now I'm right beside them. I'm yelling at the killer, but he doesn't see me or hear me."

A few seconds passed, then Monica piped in. "The killer is straddling her now. You still think the woman is someone else because he has her on her stomach and you can't see her face."

"Yes. He's talking to the woman, telling her he doesn't want to kill her and that it's his mother who wants her dead.

And then, and then . . ."

"And then he cuts her," Monica finished Rachel's sentence.

"He kills her—she's lying there dying. He almost cut her head off!" Rachel shrieked. A moment passes and Rachel spoke again. "Now he's writing a message on this wooden heart. He writes '*Forgive Me.*'"

Monica chimed in. "Now he's placing the heart above the woman's head . . . he's cradling it in her hands."

"Yes. Now he's standing up. He raises his arms to the sky and starts talking to his mother," Rachel says then pauses. "He's done. He's leaving. He's crying."

"Yes," Monica says. "Now you are floating over to the body."

"All of a sudden I'm able to move my arms and legs. I'm turning her over. I'm wiping the blood off her face with my shirt and . . . and . . . do you see it now? It's my face! You see it? God, it's me! The woman he kills is me! I gotta stop, please, Monica, I have to stop," Rachel said, struggling for air, her chest heaving.

"You're done, sweetie," Monica calmly said. "You can stop now—I saw everything. Open your eyes." Rachel sighed with relief, opened her eyes, and looked at Monica. She was shocked at what she saw—Monica looked entirely different.

Gone was the vivacious woman who sat across from her just minutes ago. She was replaced by a woman who looked ten years older, wrinkles lining her washed-out pale face. She looked exhausted, haunted even. Rachel studied her face with awe at the drastic change. Monica's eyes were still closed, as if she was still processing the dream. Finally, she opened them.

"My god, Monica," Rachel blurted out. "What happened to you?"

Monica knew what she meant—it happened every time she connected with a patient who was having horrific dreams.

"I should have warned you before we started," Monica said apologetically. "Whenever I connect to a patient's dream, I enter into the patient's mind. I see their dreams just as vividly as they do and I take on all the feelings they experience during their dream. Like how you felt during this dream, you were terrified, angry, confused, helpless—all of that. I realize it is very difficult for patients to relive these types of dreams, but it is just as hard on me because I'm right there with them, reliving the dream. I am just as involved in it as you are," she explained, running her fingers through her hair, trying to catch her breath. Finally, she regained some of her composure and started to look more like herself, but certainly not entirely. It was the strangest thing Rachel had ever witnessed.

"OK, Rachel, like I said before, when someone has a dream and I connect with them, I know whether or not the person is in danger. Like I said, dream interpretation is my expertise. I'm able to determine whether the dream is, in fact, a premonition or if it's just a bad nightmare. I know what signs to look for, and my own psychic ability allows me to differentiate between the two," Monica explained.

"In your case, this is only a nightmare, nothing more. The reason you are probably having this dream is because of all the media hype about this killer." Monica sighed and threw her hands up in the air. "I mean, who isn't a little freaked out by this lunatic?"

"What about the premonition I had about the airplane dream? It seems ironic that I also had that dream every night—just as vividly—for a few weeks before the crash, and look what happened—I was right."

"Yes, Rachel, you were right about the plane crash," Monica agreed. "But that dream was different than this one."

"So you're telling me that if I would've connected with you prior to the plane crash, you would've known it was a premonition and not just a bad dream?" Rachel asked.

"That is correct. I would have known that it was a valid premonition and that you were, in fact, in danger," Monica explained. "Rachel, I know you may be worried, but please, trust me on this. You are safe. Like I said, I have worked with hundreds of people who have come to me with this kind of situation. Sometimes they will walk away just as skeptical as you seem to be right now. It is what it is—it's just a bad dream, nothing more, nothing less."

Rachel's bottom lip started to quiver. "I don't know . . . this dream is just as vivid as the plane crash dream was. I don't see what the difference would be."

"One major difference is that, in the plane crash dream, you actually experienced the crash *through the eyes of a passenger* on the plane. *You were* the passenger. In this murder dream, you are not actually *experiencing* the murder through the eyes of the woman getting murdered. You are a third party *watching* the murder take place. Does that make sense?"

"I see what you are saying, but in my book, dead is dead. That woman lying there butchered on the forest floor is me."

"Don't let it worry you. I would know if it was a premonition, and it's not," Monica said persuasively.

"OK," Rachel said skeptically.

After she scratched out the check and handed it to Monica, she struggled to get herself up out of the chair. When she finally did, she headed for the door. With her back toward Monica, she stopped and turned back around. "I hope you're right, because my life depends on it," she said with an uncertain voice, and then she left.

"I hope you're right, because my life depends on it." Rachel's words chilled Monica to the core, and she sat shrouded in doubt for the first time in years. Those *exact* words were spoken by someone else decades ago. The incident had remained dormant at the fringes of Monica's mind until now. After all these years, the veil lifted and the memory came screaming back.

Monica had connected with a man who was also having dreams about his own death. She had also assured him, like Rachel, that he was just having nightmares and that he was safe. He wasn't. It was the only time Monica had been wrong and it cost the man his life. His death had created a significant chink in Monica's psychic armor of confidence then, and now her confidence had been shaken again.

Her client had been found murdered in his apartment three days after his session with Monica. It had been a gunshot wound to the head—just as in his dream. The force that wanted his fate sealed had tricked Monica—a trick that resulted in a deadly outcome. How did she make that mistake? Why didn't she feel the strong, negative force that accompanies a premonition? Why didn't she see the difference? At that time, the guilt almost destroyed her. She may as well have been the one to point the gun to the man's head and pulled the trigger.

Chapter 6

Randall Metzgar was a drifter who never touched down in any one area long enough to stir up any suspicion for his crimes. He worked odd jobs to make just enough money to eat and kill. He was living in an old dilapidated apartment complex that sat on the corner of Fifth and Central in one of the most dangerous parts of south Seattle.

The old, red brick apartment building was run down from years of neglect. Cracked cement fell randomly on to the pavement below, creating a hazardous environment for anyone who dared to walk by. Dumpsters were lined along the back of the building, convenient for bums to scavenge through for their next meal. As a result, garbage was strewn everywhere. A putrid stench wafted through the air.

Skanky hookers lined Pacific Highway South with their flashy "barely there" attire and their ridiculously glittered high heeled shoes that lured men with every step. Every once in a while, a pimp could be seen shouting and shoving a prostitute. No one would dare come to the prostitute's rescue—not if they valued their life. Confrontation would be like playing Russian roulette with all six bullets in the chamber. Everyone just knew to turn their heads and not interfere. Drive-by shootings drove numerous innocent people to early graves. Gangs ruled the streets, and people who foolishly roamed into dark alleys on the wrong night and at the wrong time may never be seen or heard from again.

The five-hundred-square-foot studio that Randall occupied smelled of smoke and sweat. One single lightbulb hung from the ceiling, casting an eerie greenish gloom throughout. In one corner was a black-and-white television that sat on top of a TV tray. In another corner, a mound of dirty clothes, most of them stained with blood. Shoved up against one wall was a badly stained twin-sized mattress with only one threadbare red blanket wadded up at the end. No pillow. Opposite the makeshift bed sat an old, small dresser riddled with stains and chips from both childhood neglect as well as the passage of time.

There was nothing on top of the dresser except one photo housed in a tarnished frame. The original black-and-white exposure was severely faded and yellowed. It was an old photo, but the woman in it radiated an angelic glow, as if it were taken yesterday. Her features were perfect, and her long blonde hair cascaded down one slim shoulder. His mother's eyes, although captured in another place and time, were able to transcend the years because they followed him.

Always.

Randall had ruined his mother, and he hated himself for it. Because of his mistake, he was now just her puppet on a string. From where she sat on the dresser, his mother was able to control his every thought, his every decision, his every move. As much as he hated being trapped in her web and under her spell, he knew he deserved her hatred, and he would never escape it unless he granted her wishes.

Her frozen smile looked innocent, but he knew better. Behind those fine, feminine lips simmered acid. He would have done anything to be able to turn back time to make her alive and pretty again, but he couldn't.

Not only had he killed his mother in such a horrific way, along with it, he had killed all the spirit his father ever had. Before the accident, Randall's relationship with his father had been good. After his mother's death, his father had beaten him repeatedly, screaming blame on him. He had even come at him with a knife, and the aftermath of that particular assault had left his face scarred. Not only was he abused physically, he was tormented with verbal abuse as well.

'You stupid, stupid idiot . . . how could you have done this to her—to me? You should have been the one who died, not her!'

The only silver lining in the black aura he carried now was that his father was now dead.

He still had a chance with his mother, he reminded himself—even from the grave. He would make it up to her. She wouldn't hate him forever if he did what she wanted him to do. He assured himself of that. Someday she would love him again.

There were times it felt like he couldn't go on. He even thought of dropping her picture from his window to watch his guilt shatter into a million tiny pieces, but he knew better. That would only anger her more and make her hatred escalate. The constant scolding and ridicule that pulsated within his head would only become louder, make her angrier. It would eventually become so intense that it would drive him into madness.

A day never escaped him without reliving the accident again and again in his mind. Randall berated himself for not listening to her the night the accident happened so many years ago. He was only eight, but he was old enough to know better.

The pull of his childhood obsession with fire had been stronger than abiding by his mother's warnings not to play with it. It was too fascinating. It lured him in like a seductress. That night, his father had been out of town on business, which was good, and it was even better that he had left some matches on the kitchen counter.

Randall's mother was fast asleep. He was in his bedroom alone with his door shut. *She won't know*, he assured himself. *She's asleep*. It was safe now. There it was—the heat, the warmth, the way it flickered so gently with his slight breath. It entranced him. He was mesmerized by how it turned his pitch black bedroom into an orange glow.

Then he accidentally dropped the lit match—a split-second mistake that changed his life forever. Why did he let it fall from his hand? Why did it hit the linen curtains as it fell? Why couldn't he stop the fire from spreading? Why had he been so careless in the first place?

Within seconds, the house was an inferno, and flames licked the sky a hundred feet high. He was able to escape, but his mother didn't. The flame that just hours ago had been his friend was now his eternal enemy. She was trapped—burning alive inside. The rescuers were finally able to pull her from the house, but she was motionless—a lifeless corpse. Her once beautiful ivory skin was now charred black and sloughing off in sheets.

As the rescuers placed her on the ground, her neck jarred and her head rolled directly toward him. What was left of her face was hideous. All her facial features were basically gone—her eyes, her ears, her hair. Her long graceful fingers were now just nubs. He knew that night that all the love she had ever had for him melted away right along with her.

He ran to the side of the bushes, horrified by what he saw, and vomited. It was surreal, yet he knew it was real. Something he could never take back. It was that night that she first asked him through lips she no longer had.

'Why, Randall? Why did you do this to me when I loved you so much?'

He picked up the picture in one trembling hand, sat down on the grungy mattress, and just stared at her. She looked at him with eyes that mirrored his own. He started to rock his massive body back and forth, his face contorting. The whimpering that came from him defied every inch of his six-feet-four frame. "Yes, Mother," he cried. "You were beautiful and alive, and I ruined you."

'Then take it away from them! Why would you let them live when you have killed me—your own mother? I was once alive and beautiful too, Randall, but you took that all away from me, remember? So why do you betray me by letting other beautiful women live? Are you just going to do nothing while they try to replace me? They mean nothing to you—and you certainly mean nothing to them. I loved you with all my heart, Randall. If you still love me, then show me! Put them where I am—in a cold dark grave so they can rot into a putrid corpse just as I have. Kill them, Randall, just like you killed me!'

He found himself studying his boots. Like two sponges, they had soaked up the blood spilled from each of his victims. Still, he would rather look at those boots for eternity than have to raise his head and look at her again.

Randall felt her glare penetrating him like venom. "Please don't make me do it again, Mother," he pleaded with tears streaming down his rugged face. He covered his ears with his giant hands, hands that had committed unthinkable crimes in an attempt to quiet her voice—quiet his madness. His head began to pound with excruciating pain just as it always did when she spoke to him.

Exhausted and in unbearable pain, his body slumped with defeat and reluctantly he succumbed to her wish—as always. "OK, Mother, I will do it again. I will do it again for you."

He had to prepare himself for the kill by mentally separating himself from the ruthless killer he must become—the killer his mother wanted him to be. He was forced to succumb to the dark sadistic thoughts that recklessly race through the mind of a true killer. He had learned how to allow the thoughts to escalate to the point of making him, like all other killers, as volatile as a house of cards. It was then, and only then, that he could turn into someone he was never meant to be—a heartless, cold-blooded monster. A monster capable of slaughtering innocent women whose only flaw was that they were beautiful, just as his mother had been.

Back and forth, back and forth, he rocked. He stood up, knowing what must be done. He took her picture, raised it to his lips, and kissed her.

'*Good boy, my love,*' her voice echoed in his mind.

He gently placed the picture back on the dresser and turned to leave. He walked toward the door, knowing his boots would soak up more blood tonight. As soon as he put his hand on the doorknob, he sensed it—her black eyes burned into the very essence of his soul.

Chapter 7

Lisa Connelly was absolutely breathtaking. Her thick shoulder—length chestnut-colored hair seemed to fall into place on its own—even when she had just rolled out of bed. She had never experienced a *bad hair day*. She was one of those anomalies who could wear very little makeup and still be a knockout. She dressed impeccably with expensive suits that accentuated her womanly figure nicely.

Her feminine facial features were soft, but strong enough to command authority. Her dark blue eyes and sultry voice captured thousands of viewers, and ratings had soared ever since she had taken over as lead anchor on the evening news.

Growing up, her parents were news junkies—the television continuously blared out stories. When she was six years old, she peered up at the TV that was broadcasting a story about a horse that had fallen through an iced-over lake. Strangely, she was more interested in the person talking about the story than the poor horse itself.

"Mommy, I want to be one of those people," she had said, pointing to the anchor. Since that time, her main goal in life was to become one. She was on the fast track and nothing was going to get in her way. She was unstoppable.

Lisa knew her looks alone would not carry her completely. She would have to have a lot more than that to make it in such a dog-eat-dog industry. She would have to fight and be more than just another pretty face to get to the top. Nothing was promised.

Lisa had started her career as a field reporter in Pasco, Washington, a small market in eastern Washington. Like any other aspiring news anchor, she had to pay her dues. Her salary was low and she barely scraped by, but she reminded herself that Pasco was only temporary and it was a necessary evil—a place where mistakes could be made.

Lisa grew a tougher skin by welcoming the coverage of gruesome car accidents, fires, drownings, and many other grim tragedies the world spits out every day. She didn't allow herself to be haunted by the horrific images she had witnessed. It was only because of her strong will to succeed that she was able to compartmentalize her professional life from her personal one. Time for an active personal life was limited. Even when she was off the clock, she found herself at the station researching and digging up potential stories—whatever it took to forge ahead. It paid off. After one year, she took a position in Spokane, Washington, a midsized market.

The money was better, but still not great. She worked there for a few years as a reporter and a part-time anchor. She sunk her teeth into her work, and a few years later, she accepted an offer from the news director at one of the major networks in Seattle as co-anchor of the evening news. The money was now rolling in nicely. *Only one more step,* she reminded herself daily. One more jump to the national level where she would reach the top and achieve her dream—hopefully before the age of thirty-five.

The success, however, had come with a price. Lisa's friends harped on her, telling her she was a workaholic, and they were right. Trying to find a balance between work and play was still a challenge for her. Prying herself away from her work was like pulling gum off the bottom of a shoe. Unfortunately, her friends had to take a backseat. And when it came to dating . . . well, that was just simply out of the question.

At the age of thirty, her friends—most of them married with kids—warned her that her baby clock was ticking and her window of opportunity to become a mother was closing in. She would remind her friends that she would have to get married before the baby, and the thought of that step scared the hell out of her. Lisa didn't want a husband or a baby to get in the way of her lifelong goal. It would be at least ten years, if at all, before she thought of building a family.

Lisa's day had been more stressful than usual, and when she headed out of the station, she was exhausted. The best solution to her situation was a nice, relaxing hot bath. She visualized the entire experience as she walked to her car—lying in her large soaker tub with a glass or two or three of wine. "Sorry, girlfriends," she murmured. "No room for a man in my tub."

She shivered as the cold breeze whipped up her hair into what felt like icy fingers tickling her face. She was thankful that as frigid as it was, at least the snow had stopped flying. Snow was beautiful, but she preferred its beauty from inside, sitting in front of a crackling fire, sipping a delectable warm cup of eggnog with an extra shot of rum. She fantasized about the slow slide of alcohol running down her throat. *On a winter's night, what could be better than that?*

Lisa had to admit that she did drink a little too much, but that was her way of quieting the demons that whirled within her. She was a perfectionist with a "slight twist" of obsessive compulsiveness. Everyone else considered her "slight twist" to be a "hard corkscrew." She tried to hide that side of her from most people, but she couldn't help but be noticed at work when she walked around straightening and smoothing everything in her office, from the papers and office paraphernalia that occupied her desk to the fringe of the rug on the floor.

It irritated her when her coworkers recklessly tossed papers on her desk. Whenever she walked into her office and her desk looked like a tornado touched down, her anxiety would rise and she would have to straighten and organize before she would let herself sit down. The papers needed to be put into neat little stacks resting at a ninety-degree angle from the edge of her desk and categorized by priority and subject. Half the time, her stapler was askew. It irritated her that her coworkers couldn't put it back precisely where it belonged.

Everyone else at her work seemed to be comfortable working in chaos and disarray. You'd be lucky if you could find one square inch of exposed wood underneath the mess of her coworkers' desks. After a while, she realized she had to choose her battles and learned to bite her tongue to keep the peace. She had given up on her quest to change people into enjoying the benefit of her ways and had learned to work with them in spite of their weaknesses. In her opinion, organization was one trait that separated her from the rest, and as a result, had catapulted her over them to where she was today.

Randall had been watching Lisa from a distance for a month now and knew her daily routine. He knew when she went to work and would often wait to see when she arrived home. It was a slight inconvenience when she decided to sell her house. Randall had spent a great deal of time inspecting it and had already figured out a plan on how he was going to break in. But once the "For Sale" sign went up, he decided to delay his plan until she was settled into her new residence. After her house sold, he had to find out where her new location was. It wasn't hard. All he had to do was follow her one night to her soon-to-be new house.

On moving day, Randall watched the men carry boxes from a large moving van into the house. She didn't know it yet, but the house would soon become her tomb. Randall noticed that the only thing Lisa lifted during her move was her index finger, telling the movers how to do their job more efficiently. She was like a queen ant telling her worker ants how to get the job done in the most efficient way. She had the finesse of a drill sergeant when she shouted out her demands. Maximum efficiency was another trait that separated her from the rest of the human race, and moving was no exception. She was orchestrating a perfectly methodical assembly line.

The move started early one morning and should have been completed in one day, but wasn't. Randall surmised that this was most likely because the worker ants had to satisfy her meticulous directions. The men seemed to comply without any problem. They were probably too enamored with her looks or scared of her sharp tone to do anything other than what she demanded.

After Lisa had settled in, Randall decided it was time to scope out the house while she was at work. He needed to figure out the best way to get in. Behind the house and under the deck, he found a window that sat low to the ground. He thought the placement of the window was odd, but it would certainly make it easier for him to enter the house. He didn't notice at first, but upon closer inspection, he realized the window was unlocked. *Even better.* He wouldn't have to break or jar the window to get in.

The movers had stacked boxes up against the interior wall, completely covering the window. Lisa must've not known about the window because otherwise it would have been securely closed and locked. He had studied Lisa long enough to know she wasn't the type to overlook something like an unlocked window.

Randall slid the window open a few inches and put his foot against a box labeled "Basement." It barely moved. This would create a problem. The boxes must be stacked quite deep and wide if he couldn't even get the box to budge. He would probably have to burrow through several of them. Being as large as he was, it would not be easy for him to squeeze through, but he could do it—it would just take time. He would come back tomorrow. Lisa had one day left to live.

Randall wasn't sure how long it was going to take to get through the boxes, so he arrived a few hours before Lisa would be home from work.

He didn't want to feel pressured for time. Pressure creates mistakes, and mistakes were not allowed.

He wasn't concerned about being seen—the winter afternoon had welcomed the premature inky sky and the backyard was covered almost entirely by foliage. He was more concerned with the noise the boxes would make as they toppled down. He needed to figure out how he could do it quietly, which meant leaving as many of the boxes undisturbed as possible. Still, because of the way the boxes were stacked, he would have to push several aside to tunnel his way through.

He opened the window, then with a forceful kick, shoved the first box aside. Boxes started cascading down, and within a half an hour he was in. He sat down quietly in Lisa's basement and waited. The waiting was the hardest part. It gave him time to think about what he had to do, which allowed his anguish to build. The tension escalated in him like a time bomb—memories of his dead mother flipped through his mind like a gory slide show. He wondered what his life would have turned out like if he had never dropped that match, never killed his mother. If that were the case, he wouldn't be sitting here now, planning out Lisa's savage death.

The ice crunching from the weight of Lisa's car sounded like tiny bones snapping as she pulled into her driveway. The weather was extremely unusual for November, but winter had come in early with a vengeance, bringing with it a blanket of snow and ice that had originally been predicted by the local weatherman to be just a temporary "cold snap." The predicted "cold snap" had plummeted temperatures well below freezing and had decided to hang around like an unwelcome relative for nearly three weeks.

The kids had even grown weary of the bitter temperatures. At first, the neighborhood was a magical winter wonderland. Dozens of children could be seen scurrying around in their puffy coats and funky looking snow hats. Now, the outdoors was like a ghost town—the snow lying undisturbed. The snowmen had taken up final residence in yards, and there was still enough snow lying around to pummel the local weatherman for his faulty forecast. Even the snow angels, in spite of their wide wing span, had decided not to take flight back to heaven.

Chapter 8

Rachel watched helplessly from where she was perched.

Lisa turned the water on in the bathtub, adding some bubble bath and sea salts. Then she sauntered into the kitchen in her nice, comfy, oversized pink plush robe. She opened up the refrigerator and her eyes focused in on what she had been waiting for all day—a bottle of nice, chilled Chateau Ste. Michelle Riesling. She uncorked it and watched the wine splash into the oversized glass she had set out that morning. Taking a sip, she felt the sweet liquid slide down her throat like smooth velvet.

Lisa picked up the glass with one hand and the bottle with the other, and headed back to the bathroom—the tub almost overflowing with bubbles. She placed the wine down on the tile that surrounded the back of the tub and dipped her finger in the water to make sure it was hot enough for her. In her opinion, hot meant what would be considered scalding by most. The hotter the better. She took the matches from the pocket of her robe and lit four candles that surrounded the tub. She had picked up the candles at a new specialty shop, the kind of place that sells aroma therapy candles along with big fluffy pillows and wicker furniture—stuff that no one really needs but buys anyway.

She had chosen the cinnamon candles for a very special reason. She had lost her mother to breast cancer three years ago. The subtle aroma that emanated from the candles reminded her of how her mother's cinnamon rolls were the best on the planet.

She flipped the radio to a soft jazz station, lowered the volume, turned off the lights, let her robe slip off and stepped into her utopia. She used all her senses to revel in it—smelling the cinnamon; feeling the hot water, the bubbles tickling against her skin; hearing the soft jazz; tasting the chilled wine. When she decided the atmosphere was perfect, she then closed her eyes, leaned back onto the small green terry cloth tub pillow and finally relaxed. A perfect ending to a stressful day.

Randall heard the water running and figured Lisa was probably preparing a bath. When he heard the water stop and her scuffling quiet down, he knew it was time. Her life would end minutes from now. As he slowly climbed the stairs, he repeated the only words that would allow him to carry out his plan: "I am a kind man, a gentle man." He quietly moved toward the softly humming music of the radio.

Once again, Rachel remained trapped in her bubble above the scene. "Stop! Stop!" The words tumbled silently out of Rachel's mouth. "Nooo!"

When Randall entered the bedroom, he saw the door to Lisa's bathroom was open about halfway. He stood there quietly and watched her from behind. Even in the dimness, he was astonished at how beautiful she was. Why did he have to be the one to take her life? She looked so innocent—totally oblivious to how vulnerable she actually was at that very moment.

He gazed at her, the soapy water gently lapping as she shifted her body. The bubbles covered most of her body, except her head. He had no interest in seeing her nude. That didn't matter to him. He never thought of his victims in a sexual way. He at least owed them that. One of Lisa's arms lazily draped over the lip of the tub. In her hand, she clutched the glass of wine. Randall watched her as she slowly swayed her head to the beat of the jazz. Her hair was carelessly clipped up on the top her head. Even so, it was beautiful.

Rachel screamed again, her lungs burning. "Please don't. Turn around and leave!" Silence. Again. She was frantic. She knew what was going to happen. There was nothing more Rachel could do or say to stop him, but still she had to try.

Randall drew a long quiet breath and made his move. He quietly knelt down behind her, grabbed her hair, and forcefully jerked her head back with one hand. She let out a shrill scream and reached back toward him in a desperate attempt to free herself. She began struggling and flailing like a freshly caught trout at the bottom of a bucket. Water and bubbles were splashing everywhere, dousing him as well as the tile floor.

The wine glass shattered, shards of it scattered onto the floor and into the tub. Randall placed one arm under her armpit and kept a hold of her hair with the other hand and pulled her out. He placed her face down on the floor—her legs wildly flailing. She screamed at such a high pitch that it hurt his ears.

"Shhh, It won't be long now," Randall quietly said. Straddling her, he grabbed both her arms and secured them under his knees. Because her body was wet and slippery, she was able to wriggle underneath him more than his other victims. But he still had her completely helpless.

"*Please . . . please,*" she gasped. "*Who are you? What do you want? Why . . . why are you doing this?*" Her lungs ached. Hot tears stung her eyes as she cried begging for her life.

"*I don't want to do this—I really don't. My mother is making me do it,*" he calmly explained. "*She has seen you on the television and she told me that you are the one she wants me to kill. I have no choice.*"

"*Let her go! Please don't do this again!*" Rachel pleaded, but knew it made no difference. She felt his feelings and heard his thoughts race through her, his mantra repeating—*I am a kind man, a gentle man.* Once again, Rachel tried to move, but she couldn't. Once again, she tried to scream out; and once again, her vocal cords were mute. She was helpless. All she could do was watch this poor woman's life come to an end.

"*Please believe me when I say I am a kind and gentle man,*" Randall said to Lisa.

"*What?*" Lisa cried, violently writhing beneath him.

"*You see, my mother was once beautiful like you, but she is dead now,*" he explained. "*She doesn't want to be replaced by other beautiful women like you. She says women like you don't deserve to live if she can't. She makes me do this as punishment because I killed her.*" He started to cry. He sobbed. "*I killed her. I killed my own mother.*"

"*You're crazy! Get off me!*" Lisa screamed. "*I'm not trying to replace anyone!*"

"*My little darling,*" he whispered. "*This is how she wants me to do it. I'm so, so sorry. It won't take long.*"

"*Stop! Stop! Get off of me!*"

"Let her go!" Rachel's internal scream raged.

He unzipped the death pack and took out the knife. He lifted her head, placed the knife below one ear, and sliced all the way across to the other ear. Blood started spewing everywhere.

Rachel wept. "You son of a bitch!"

With Lisa's hair still in his grip, Randall dropped the knife and leaned toward her face with closed eyes. He let her warm blood pulsate onto his face, "I am sorry. You don't know how very sorry I am. Please forgive me. But I will stay with you. I won't let you die alone. I'll take your blood with me." When her body slumped beneath him, he knew she was dead.

"It's all over, my love. You will suffer no more," he said, soothing her corpse as if she could still hear him. He sat back up and gently slid his gloved hand through her wet, bloody hair. Reaching into his pack, he pulled out the other items. He used the rag to wipe his face then picked up the black marker and wrote "Forgive Me" on the wooden heart. Positioning it above Lisa's head, he raised her arms and placed the heart between her hands.

"You sick son of a bitch!" Rachel strained.

Randall then stood up and flipped the light switch on. He wanted to revel at how beautiful Lisa was in the full light. Even from behind, without her face visible—even with the blood, her body emanated such perfection, such beauty. His mother would be proud. But he thought it sad that the bubbles still left in the bath tub had been less fragile than she.

Rachel finally started floating down to the scene. She stood next to Randall raging. She studied his face closely now that she could see it in the full light. Large brown eyes without a glint of evil in them. His nose was long and broad, which would probably look too big on most people. But for some reason, it suited him nicely. Lips that were thick and quivering. He made no attempt to hide his scar with facial hair, and although most of his head was covered with a knit black cap, she could tell his hair was dark brown and wavy.

How could such a pleasant face belong to someone so savage, so ruthless? His face looked like it should belong to that of a true and sensitive man—like a man who would feel bad after accidentally stepping on an ant.

Randall couldn't turn back time—it was done. The despair built in him like an unforgiving tidal wave. Now for some reason, he questioned himself for the first time on fault. The gruesome scene splayed out before him was none other than the result of a grisly act of murder created by his own hand—a detached brutality.

Randall looked up to the ceiling and spoke, "It's you, Mother. You are the reason for all of this!" Even though angry, he found comfort in knowing that his love for his mother ran deep enough to do anything for her—including becoming someone he was not.

After Randall left the room, Rachel floated over to the woman. She was able to move her hands freely now, so she rolled the woman over. She grabbed a towel and wiped the blood off her face. She looked familiar, but Rachel couldn't remember from where. She gently laid the woman's head back down and started walking through the house, looking for any clues to identify the woman. She noticed a briefcase on the kitchen table. Inside, Rachel found business cards.

"Lisa Connelly, News Anchor."

Oh my dear god! Rachel thought to herself. Lisa Connelly . . . she watched her all the time on television.

"Don't worry, Lisa, I will make sure he suffers for this," she murmured.

With inexplicable rage, Rachel suddenly woke up, shouting the words, "I've got you, you bastard. I know your face!" With her hands shaking and her whole body quivering, Rachel grabbed the phone with a trembling hand and dialed Monica's number off the napkin she had placed on her nightstand.

Monica picked up on the second ring. "There's going to be another murder!" Rachel shouted.

"Go on," Monica responded, confused.

"I had a dream last night, but it wasn't about me this time. The Heartbreak Killer is going to kill another woman," Rachel said, trying to catch her breath.

"Rachel . . ." Monica tried to intervene.

"Wait—I know you don't think I'm in danger, but someone else is."

"Rachel, like I told you before, you are just having nightmares. That's all they are."

"Monica, I know that's what you think they are, but I can't live with myself if someone doesn't warn this woman," Rachel panted. "Just please, please meet with me again and we'll know for sure."

"Rachel, it doesn't work like that. I can only tell if the dream is a premonition if I connect with the person who is having the dream," Monica explained.

"Please, Monica, I won't be able to live with myself if we don't at least try," Rachel pleaded.

"Did you see the woman's face clearly?" Monica asked.

"Yes . . . very. You're not going to believe who it is . . . it's—"

Monica cut her off, "Don't tell me. It will help if you don't tell me who she is. I have an opening in an hour, will that work?" Monica asked.

"I'll make it work . . . thank you," Rachel said.

"I can't promise you anything, Rachel. Remember that," Monica warned.

"I know that, but we have to try."

Rachel didn't have time to shower. Instead, she threw on her ivory cable sweater and an old pair of jeans. She grabbed her jacket, purse, and car keys, and was out the door in less than twenty minutes.

Rachel settled into the big huggable love seat, and once again, it claimed her body. Monica sat beside her. "You know the drill," Monica said as she extended her hands out toward Rachel. "Remember to concentrate. Don't think of anything else except what you saw in your dream."

After what seemed like an eternity to Rachel, Monica finally spoke. "I see him now."

"He's going to murder her . . . she's going to die! Do you see who the woman is?" Rachel chimed in.

"Shhh," Monica interrupted. "It's best you don't tell me who she is. I will know soon enough." A few seconds passed and then Monica said, "He's waiting for her in a basement it looks like . . ."

"Yes, he's . . . ," Rachel blurted out.

"Shhh, let me see it on my own."

Rachel, though irritated, became silent.

"She's preparing a bath for herself," Monica said. After a minute or so, Monica continued, "He's climbing the stairs. More time passed and then she said, "Now he's pulling her out of the bathtub."

"Yes!" Rachel cried.

Finally, Monica spoke again, "He's talking to her. He's telling her how sorry he is . . ." Another pause. "The way he is killing her is the same as in your other dream. He has her on her stomach and now . . . oh god." Monica stopped speaking to take a deep breath. "He sliced her."

"Yes! He's crazy!" Rachel said.

A moment later, Monica said, "He's placing the heart between her hands just like in your other dream. Yes, it looks like the same guy."

Rachel continued to focus on the dream as she saw it, visualizing the part when she found Lisa's business card.

"It's Lisa Connelly, the news anchor," Monica said.

"Yes, yes, see . . ."

"OK, Rachel, that's good. You can stop now."

"She's going to be his next victim!" Rachel cried, her eyes wild.

Monica looked at her intently. "Rachel, again, this is a very vivid and horrible dream, but it doesn't mean it's going to happen."

"What? We've got to at least warn her! This dream isn't about me. This is about someone else. You saw how he murders her. You saw everything I did!" Rachel replied angrily.

"Yes, I saw everything you saw, but that's what I do—I'm a psychic. Just because I saw your dream doesn't necessarily mean anything alarming. It's a dream, Rachel. That's all."

Rachel was steaming and felt her mouth tighten and her face redden. "For the love of God! How can you deny this?"

"Like I told you on the phone, I can only tell if someone's dream is a premonition if I connect with the person who is having the dream. You're not Lisa Connelly, Rachel. It would be different if Lisa had come to me with this dream. I would then be able to connect with her to determine if this dream is a premonition or just a nightmare."

"Dammit, Monica, we need to warn her!" Rachel hissed, narrowing her eyes. "I'm not going to live with the same guilt about this as I do about the plane crash."

Monica sighed in frustration. "Rachel, I tell people how I see things and what I believe no matter how much my clients may believe otherwise. Do you think I would still be in business if I translated things inaccurately? That's why people trust me—that's why the police feel I'm credible enough to help them out. I am seeing *your* dream, not *Lisa's* dream," she said, folding her hands.

"She's a news anchor. You've been watching her on television. She's been reporting about this killer all along. You've probably just subconsciously jumbled the two together," she explained.

"I can't believe you're not more alarmed!"

"I would be more worried if Lisa was the one telling me this instead of you."

This inflamed Rachel. "Oh you would be worried about her? You're certainly not worried about me getting murdered! What's the difference?"

"I know when someone is in danger. I can tell you for certain that you are *not* in danger. I can't know if Lisa is in danger because I'm not connecting with her. Doesn't that make sense to you?"

Rachel glared at Monica, shaking her head. She stood up and began walking toward the door. "You're impossible! I think you're going to be sorry about this. Two more people are going to end up dead—me being one of them and Lisa being the other. Let me remind you, Monica, that apparently, I'm psychic too—remember? You said so yourself," she huffed. "You may not have the instinct or feeling—or whatever the hell you call it—but I do. I have no doubt this will happen. It's gonna happen to me. It's gonna happen to Lisa, and when it does . . . ," Rachel said, pointing her finger at Monica. "May God help you." She turned and walked out, slamming the door behind her.

Chapter 9

Rachel pulled up to the familiar house on the corner. The red brick house was old, weathered, yet very quaint. It was located in West Seattle—an area known for old unique homes, some dating as far back as the 1930s. Many of the homes had been remodeled, but some still held the charm from nearly half a century ago.

Rachel's parents bought the house back in the seventies when they moved from Alabama. Although charming, it was in desperate need of some renovation—new paint, new roof, new masonry work on the outside, and new hardwood floors on the inside. Still, whenever Rachel walked into her parents' house, the warm comforting feeling would fill her heart. Snug and cozy. It was a calm place, a sanctuary—and absolutely overflowing with peace and love.

Carl swung the door open, wearing his infamous smile—big, wide, and toothy. "Happy Thanksgiving! How's my baby girl?" He said, stepping forward to give Rachel a huge bear hug, a trait he was known for.

Carl was a large man with unruly thick white hair, a well-groomed beard, and green eyes. He had muscular arms and legs from years of working on a farm and stood a good foot taller than her mother. Rachel always thought it looked so cute every time her parents kissed because Carl had to lean down as Anita stood up on her tippy toes to reach him.

"Hi, Daddy," Rachel responded, gasping after having the air squeezed out of her. "Gosh, Dad, you nearly made me drop the pie!"

"I'm sorry, honey. What would Thanksgiving be without the pumpkin pie? C'mon in and join us," he said, putting his huge hand on the small of her back. The aroma of turkey, mashed potatoes, and gravy filled the house. Her mom was a wonderful cook and having dinner with her parents was always a treat, but Thanksgiving was unbelievable.

Rachel walked into the small kitchen and set her purse and the pie down on the country-style round table that was covered with a red-and-white checkered table cloth. Her mother turned from the stove and took off her oven mitt to give Rachel a hug. Rachel wrapped her arms around her mother's wide girth. Her arms weren't quite long enough to wrap completely around her due to the fact that Anita was about as round as she was tall.

"Hi, Mama," she said, giving her mom a big kiss on her warm, rosy, chubby cheek. Anita looked like a professional chef with food remnants splashed across her apron. She had been working for hours preparing the feast for the people she loved most.

"Oh I am so glad to see you!" Anita gushed.

"Mama, everything smells so good. You are such a good cook. You certainly know that I'm not. Remember the year I attempted to do Thanksgiving dinner?" Rachel grimaced then laughed. "What a disaster." Cooking was something her mother had always tried to get Rachel interested in, but to no avail. She was not the domestic type and doubted she ever would be.

"Oh stop it, your pumpkin pies are the best in this world," Anita said, bending down to inspect it, gently touching the crust.

"Yeah, Daddy almost made me drop it on the way in. Good thing I didn't. As we all know, it's the only thing I can make," Rachel declared.

Anita quickly came to her defense. "So what if you aren't domesticated? You are a career woman!" For some strange reason, her mother's comment made her think about Billy Cooper—the student from hell. A wave of nausea churned in her stomach.

Rachel noticed the pecan pie her mother already had sitting on the kitchen counter. "Mmm . . . ," Rachel purred. "Pecan pie—my favorite."

Anita reached out and cradled Rachel's face in her hands and patted one cheek. "Now the only thing we need to do is find your favorite man."

Here we go again, Rachel thought.

"You know, there are some wonderful single men at my church—some of them quite handsome." She winked at Rachel. "Why don't you join me this Sunday and then you can see for yourself." Rachel just hugged her back without replying. She didn't want to get her mom started on the subject of her love life, or lack thereof.

Anita had set her up before on a few dates in the past, which ended up as complete disasters. Her mother's idea of a good future husband was completely opposite of what Rachel envisioned. Anita pulled back and locked eyes with Rachel's. "Next Sunday, you meet me here at 8:30."

Oh dear Lord, how am I going to get out of this one?

"Maybe, Mom, maybe," Rachel replied, noticing the lines etched in her mother's face. In spite of it all, she knew her mother's intentions were all good. "I love you, Mom."

"Not as much as I love you . . . to the moon and back," Anita commented, referring to Rachel's favorite childhood bedtime story, *Goodnight Moon.*

"C'mon, girls, enough of that mushy stuff, let's get this table set," Carl said, walking into the kitchen.

"OK, Daddy. I was just telling Mama how much I loved her. And I love you just as much," she said, giving him a hug that paled in comparison to his.

When Rachel opened the silverware drawer, she heard the boys running up the stairs like a herd of elephants squealing with delight. "Oh my god, you got them—the boys!"

Anita's face broke out into a smile of pleasure that was as vast as it was wide when the boys screamed into the kitchen. "There you two are. You need to meet my baby girl, Rachel."

Both boys walked up to Rachel with perplexed expressions. "She's not a baby," one of the boys said, cocking his head as he stared at Rachel.

"She looks pretty old to me," the other twin said. Both Rachel and Anita laughed. Bending down to their level Rachel said, "I'm *really, really* old."

They both continued to stare at her with curious huge identical brown eyes blessed with long camel-like lashes. Long lashes—a trait Rachel had always wished she'd had. It was a frustration she was reminded of every time she put her mascara on. Why was it that boys seemed to be blessed with gorgeous lashes that should be reserved for the female species?

"So now, who are you?" Rachel asked, addressing one of the twins.

"I'm Preston," the boy blurted out.

"And I'm Austin," the other one said, slapping his hands to his chest.

"And how old are you?" Rachel's asked. Both boys held up five fingers.

Rachel's eyes glanced from one to the other in astonishment at how much they looked alike—what a peculiar thing it must be to have a complete replica of yourself. She could not imagine it. She was bewildered at how every little expression, laugh, and physical characteristic completely mirrored the other.

"Now can we go back downstairs to watch cartoons and play with our trucks?" Preston asked Anita.

She put her hand on his head, messing up his hair, "Yes . . . you may. But dinner will be ready in just a few minutes." Before she had finished her answer, they were already racing down the stairs.

"They're good boys," Anita said, smiling. Suddenly, her eyes changed to an expression of sadness—something that Rachel didn't see very often in her mother. "They have been through a lot," she said as tears started welling up in her round blue eyes. "They had a horrible mother and no known father. It's too bad I couldn't have gotten them as babies. I just hope the scars don't run too deep."

"I'm sure that whatever scars they may have, you and Dad will do an awesome job smoothing them out," Rachel consoled, wrapping her arm around her mother again. Anita wiped her eyes. Rachel saw her mother's solemn expression slowly transition back into a smile.

"Now, darling," her mother said, studying Rachel's face. "What's going on with you? You look kinda tired, honey. Is everything OK?"

"Yeah, yeah—things are great," Rachel lied, conjuring up as much positivity as she could muster.

Anita looked suspiciously at her. "You sure?"

"Mom, I'm fine," Rachel attempted again. She glanced up and saw the wooden rooster perched on top of her mother's kitchen cabinet. It stared down at her in disgust. *Liar.*

"Rachel," her mom tilted her head and put her hands on her hips, which was an indicator that her mom did not believe her. "You know you cannot fool your mother."

"Uhm," Rachel hesitated. She had never been very good with a poker face, and to make things worse, her mother had always had a sixth sense that Rachel could never fool. Rachel looked down at her feet.

Anita gently said, "C'mon, baby, I'm here for you. What is it?" She used her pointer finger to lift up Rachel's chin so she could look her straight in the eyes.

Rachel's mind was doing cartwheels, trying to conjure up a good excuse. Finally, unable to do so, she sighed. "I've just had some troubling dreams, that's all." Rachel prayed her mother wouldn't go into her ritualistic intense questioning—questions that Rachel didn't want to answer.

"What kind of dreams, honey," Anita asked, concerned.

Great. Here we go. "Oh, stupid dreams—you know, just stupid scary dreams," Rachel smiled, hoping her mother would just accept that answer at face value. "It's no big deal, Mom. Everyone has bad dreams, right?"

"I suppose, but what are the dreams about? They don't sound like stupid dreams if they are causing you concern," Anita brushed a soothing hand along Rachel's face.

"I'm sure it's nothing, Mom. It's probably just something to do with those terrible serial killer books I read or the horror movies I watch. You know, it's probably my own fault. Just my imagination going nuts."

"What are the dreams about?" her mother continued to probe.

Rachel tried to avoid the question. "Mom, it's really no big deal."

"Rachel Jo Carter, tell me what they are about!" her mother responded impatiently.

"OK, OK!" she finally conceded. "I'm having really vivid dreams about this man chasing me through a forest and killing me . . . jeez, Mom, you don't need to know about something this trivial." Rachel decided not to mention that the man chasing her was the notorious Heartbreak Killer.

"Oh my. How many times have you had this dream?"

"Several times," Rachel responded reluctantly, thinking she should've lied. Again.

"Several times, meaning what? Once a week? Every couple of days? Every day?" Anita pried.

Rachel really considered lying this time, but knew that her mother and her sixth sense would pick up on it. "Every night for the past two weeks."

"Oh my," Anita responded, the lines etched in her face deepening. "Every night! No wonder you are stressed out."

"That's why I didn't want to tell you. It's nothing—just stupid crazy dreams, so don't worry. I don't want you to get upset over this, Mom."

"I worry because I am your mother. You'll see. One day, when you have your own children, you'll worry too. Mothers worry about their kids incessantly—it's natural. Any mother who doesn't worry about her kids has her head screwed on wrong or is too selfish to have had kids in the first place."

"I know, Mom. But really, it's just a dream, OK?"

Patting Rachel on the shoulder, Anita said, "OK, Rachel, but you let me know if this continues. I'll send you home with some tea tonight. It always helps me when I start to worry about something. This tea will do the trick and calm you down." *I'll be drinking it every night,* Rachel thought to herself.

Her mother walked over to the cupboard and stepped up on her tippy toes to grab the tea that sat on the top shelf. "Here you go, dear," Anita said, handing it to her.

"Thanks, Mom."

She could feel the tears coming on. *Don't do it, don't do it,* Rachel warned herself, but It was too late. She burst out, letting all the worry over the dreams liquefy into a million tears.

"Oh, honey," Anita said, rushing to hug her daughter. "It's OK . . ."

"OK, girls," Carl's booming voice echoed throughout the kitchen as he came around the corner, quickly rubbing his hands together in excitement. "We need to finish setting the table. The bird is carved and we are ready to chow down." When he saw the two women huddled together and heard the crying, he stopped in his tracks, realizing he had just interrupted a very serious conversation.

"We'll be there in a minute," Anita said, waving him off. Carl did an about face and scurried out of the kitchen. He didn't want to get involved. He always seemed to make these types of conversations worse. His intentions were always good; he just had difficulty expressing his support when it came to women.

He was a big husky man who had strived all his life to be as hard as nails, but at the same time, wanting to be someone with a bit more sensitivity. He'd never quite figured out the correct balance. He'd grown up with seven brothers. When it came to figuring out women, he had resigned himself to realizing it would forever be a work in progress. He was just glad he had Anita who understood this and was excellent at smoothing out his rough spots.

"Let's talk about this later, Mom, OK? Let's just enjoy the day."

Her mother hesitantly agreed, handing her a paper towel to dry her tears. "Here, honey," she said with her worried expression growing deeper.

Rachel composed herself and everyone enjoyed the dinner. They chatted about the upcoming Christmas holiday. "I know what I want for Christmas," Preston said excitedly.

"And what would that be?" Rachel asked him.

"Lots of things. Things like Legos, army men, some Power Ranger stuff, uh . . . ," he said, looking up at the ceiling with his pointer finger under his chin.

"Well I want a G.I. Joe. One that comes with really cool clothes," Austin piped in.

"Yeah, G.I. Joes," Preston agreed, smiling at his brother.

Carl offered up his wide smile, looking at the two imps. "Wow, that is a lot of presents, don't you think? Do you think Santa has a bag big enough for all those toys?"

"Well he does it every year, ya know," Preston retorted back like that was the most ridiculous question he had ever heard.

"Yes, silly, he does it every year," Austin agreed, looking at Carl like he had lost his mind.

"His bag has to be big enough for everyone's toys—yeah, for everyone in the whole wide world! Enough for a zillion kids," Preston lectured Carl.

"Only for good kids though," Carl warned.

The twins looked at each other worried and said in unison, "We are good."

Anita intervened, "You boys are super. I'm sure Santa will have lots of presents stuffed in his bag for you both. And don't you worry, Santa's bag is expandable."

"Ex-can-da-ble?" Austin asked curiously.

"*Expandable.* That means it stretches and stretches so it can hold all your toys and everyone else's too," Rachel said, scrunching up her nose.

"And Santa knows how much space it will take," Preston said.

"Yeah, and Santa knows what we want," Austin added, looking at Anita confidently. "Remember we mailed him a letter with our wish list yesterday?"

"Yes you did, all the way up to the North Pole where Santa and Mrs. Claus live with all their elves," she assured them both. The boys looked at each other with big doe eyes.

"See, Santa Claus can do anything," Preston said, looking back at Carl.

"You boys are right. Being a lot older and all, I tend to forget about how magical Santa is. He can make anything happen," Carl said, winking at Rachel, reminding her that she too once believed in such things.

Once dinner was over, Anita and Rachel returned to the kitchen. "I'll be fine, Mama," Rachel assured Anita as she washed one of the china plates in the warm sudsy water.

"I surely hope so," Anita said as she swirled another plate dry with a towel. "You promise to call me if you need me, and don't forget to drink that tea. It does wonders. You know it doesn't always take a pill to fix things. These doctors like to hand out pills like candy, and sometimes all you need is a more natural remedy . . . plus there are no side effects."

It was almost seven o'clock and Rachel decided she needed to go. She leaned over and hugged both boys. She stood up and looked at them for several seconds—her eyes shifting from one boy to the other, amazed at the similarities. "OK, next time I see you boys, don't be teasing me with a game of who is who," she warned them, tweaking one nose and then the other with her thumb and pointer finger. They just giggled and ran downstairs to play.

Rachel said cheerfully, "Wow, Mom, those are two sweet little boys. It will be fun to have little carbon copies running around, don't you think? It's like they can read each other's minds." She laughed. Reaching out, she gently put her hand on Anita's arm. "You did the right thing by taking them both, Mom. If it had been me, I would've done the same thing. It would be terrible to separate them, especially because they are identical twins. From what I've heard, identical twins are linked together forever. Some people say they even know what the other is thinking, and they can feel when something is wrong with the other."

Rachel kissed her mother on the cheek and bid both her mom and dad good-bye. She then walked out into the cool, crisp air. Anita somberly watched the taillights of her daughter's car fade into the frosty night. Even when she could no longer see the car, she stood there at the window with tears welling up in her eyes. May God forgive her for what she had done.

As Rachel drove away, she couldn't shake the feeling that something wasn't right. Something was off. She didn't know what it was, but something unexplainable was tugging at her heart.

Chapter 10

Rachel woke up before her alarm clock went off, which was rare for her. She shuffled into the kitchen in her blue terry cloth robe and Mickey Mouse slippers that Heather had given her for her birthday last year. She poured water into the coffee maker and prepared a bowl of her favorite cereal. She had resorted to using fat-free milk lately. It didn't taste nearly as good as the one percent, but she was a stickler on weight. Out of fear, she hadn't been taking her daily jogs lately and didn't want to gain extra pounds. She grabbed the bowl and walked into the family room and plopped down on her comfy couch. Cali jumped up beside her to check out what she was eating, always being more interested in Rachel's food than her own. Rachel picked up the remote and turned on the television. Flipping through the channels, she finally decided on a news station. The news anchor was talking about how the president of the United States was going to cut taxes. When he was done with that story, he transitioned into a story about a new baby polar bear at the Woodland Park Zoo, and then onto a story about a dog who had saved a baby's life.

The channel cut to a commercial with a cheesy salesman talking about how great his used cars were. "Wanna buy mine?" Rachel asked the man on the TV. "It would be a steal."

The news flicked back on and then she heard it. "Sadly, all of us here at Channel Twelve regret to inform you that our news anchor, Lisa Connelly, who has been missing since Thursday, was found dead in her home last night. The police have determined that her death is the result of a homicide," the male anchor somberly reported.

Crash. Rachel sat paralyzed, soaked in cereal and milk. "Oh my dear god," she whispered. "There it is . . . there it is . . ." The story continued with the history of Lisa's career, but the television anchor's words were garbled to Rachel and sounded as if they were coming out of his mouth in slow motion. Her mind was reeling partially because she was in disbelief, and partially because she wasn't.

Now that her dream about Lisa Connelly had been confirmed, Rachel rushed to the phone to call Monica. She felt as if she had been punched in the stomach. Hopefully, Monica would believe her now.

"Monica," Rachel said in a terrified, trembling voice. "It's Rachel."

There were a few seconds of silence on the phone before Monica responded. "Yes, Rachel, hello."

"Have you heard the news about Lisa Connelly?" Rachel asked frantically.

"Yes, I did, earlier this morning. You definitely have my attention now, Rachel."

"What should we do?" Rachel asked, desperately on the verge of crying.

"I think what I need to do now is call the police and let them know what is going on. No offense, Rachel, but I think if you make the call, the police would chalk you up to another quack pretending to be a psychic for publicity. They know me. I will let them know you are legitimate," Monica responded. "I will call you once I speak with the police and let you know what the next step is. Hopefully, they'll want you to go in to the station so they can get a good sketch of what the killer looks like."

"OK. I'll wait for your call. But please, please hurry. They need to catch this psychopath before he kills me or anyone else," Rachel pleaded. "I hope you realize now that I am in great danger."

Monica was still not concerned for Rachel's safety. She would know if Rachel herself were at risk. Or would she? She still hadn't completely eradicated the doubt that clung to her since the last time she saw Rachel. To assure Rachel as well as herself, she said, "Rachel, let's not jump to conclusions. Like I said before, I genuinely think you are safe. Like I told you the other day, I would've felt danger during our connection if your dream was a premonition."

"Monica, I would give anything to believe you right now—anything, but I don't. I just have a bad feeling that I'm next."

Monica decided not to argue. "Good-bye, Rachel, I will call you soon."

Chapter 11

The morning rustling sound of backpacks being thrown on the ground beside desks and the loud din of young voices talking over each other filled the classroom and only accentuated Rachel's frayed nerves. She sat at her desk trying, without much luck, to prepare for the day. The kids finally settled down and slowly put their focus on Rachel. Some alert and smiling, some sleepy eyed, and others already bored.

The kids sensed that something was different about Rachel. One student, Marci Newburg, came up to her after class a few days ago and asked her if she was OK. She lied to her and told her she was fabulous.

Rachel had to admit that she sometimes told her students little white lies, but only when the situation warranted it. She justified that this was definitely one of those situations.

Before she could address the students, Billy Cooper was already teasing a student who was wearing a black-and-red checkered shirt.

"What are you Ronnie? A lumberjack? Are you going to cut down some trees?" Billy asked sarcastically. Ronnie's face turned as red as the fake apple on Rachel's desk. *Here we go,* Rachel thought—Billy was already ripping apart a fellow classmate. Ronnie was a shy introvert, which made him an easy target for Billy's bullying. All eyes shifted toward Ronnie, with some of the kids trying to control their laughter.

"Billy, I am not going to deal with your attitude this morning!" Rachel reprimanded. "Apologize to Ronnie right now!"

Billy shifted his body toward Ronnie. "Sorry, Ronnie," he said sarcastically.

Trying to control her tone of voice, Rachel said, "You know the rules in this classroom and at this school—no bullying."

Completely ignoring Rachel's words, Billy turned toward Ronnie again and said, "Just wait until recess, Ronnie. I'm going to yank that stupid shirt off you. I don't want to sit in the same classroom as a stupid lumberjack."

"Billy!" Rachel said, trying to reel in her temper. "That's it! You and I are going to take a little walk to Mr. Simpson's office." Rachel hurried across the classroom toward Billy's desk, but before she got to him, he used his pointer finger to gesture slitting his throat.

Rachel's face turned as white as alabaster. The other students just sat there bug-eyed, some holding their hand over their mouths in shock.

"You know you are going to die." The evil smirk on Billy's face spoke volumes. Rachel stopped dead in her tracks. Her ears started to ring and her vision started to fade. She started breaking into a sweat and then . . . *black*.

Rachel slowly felt herself returning to consciousness. She had no idea how long she'd been out. A circle of worried faces stared down at her. One of her students, Molly Hensen, was placing cold paper towels on her forehead, her eyes as big as saucers. "Are you, OK?" Molly asked Rachel, concerned.

It didn't surprise Rachel that it had been Molly nursing her back into reality. It was always Molly who took care of everyone else in their time of need. It wasn't uncommon to see her guiding an injured student to the sick room during recess.

Rachel could easily see Molly as a future nurse or doctor. Some people, like herself, knew from when they were a child what they wanted to do for a career. Molly was one of them.

Career day came to the school once a year. People from a variety of professions were invited to come speak to the class about their specialty and answer any questions the children may have. The year a nurse came in to speak, no one could get a question in sideways because Molly was firing questions at the nurse like a Gatling gun. When the nurse had finished her presentation, Molly ran after her like a pesky reporter looking for the day's scoop. The nurse didn't seem to mind, the smile on her face was as big as Molly's.

Once Rachel was coherent enough to make sound decisions, she buzzed the principal's office and asked Helen if any subs were on call for that day. She briefly explained to Helen, the office manager whom everyone knew to be the Principal's mistress, what had happened.

"No problem," Helen answered in her sweet singsong voice. "We have several on-call subs. I can probably get someone here in about fifteen minutes. You just go on home dear, lie down and rest."

Helen James was a sweet woman in her mid-forties with jet black hair that was usually piled high on top of her head. Her only flaw was that she tended to be the school's gossip queen. Helen would make sure the information that she had just become privy to would spread like wildfire. Most people didn't mind it when rumors were started by Helen because she had a heart of gold and would never spread rumors to harm or embarrass anyone. The information she shared was more out of concern and out of her protective motherly instinct. Still, Rachel was sure that by the time she returned to school tomorrow, people would be coming up to her, asking if she was pregnant or suffering from some fatal condition.

One day, Rachel had stepped into the office before heading to her classroom and saw Helen sitting at her desk, glasses perched on her nose, deep in a rag magazine that read, "Alien Spotted Jogging" on the front page. It was then clear to Rachel that Helen was an inquiring-minds-want-to-know type of person. The irony of it was that Helen was completely oblivious to the fact that the biggest gossip story of all was her affair with the principal, Mr. Simpson.

Many of the students loved Helen because she often acted as a buffer between them and the principal by convincing the principal to go easy on them. For obvious reasons, Helen had a certain amount of influence over the principal's decisions regarding disciplinary actions and would go to bat for the children.

As Rachel was driving home, she reminisced about the only other time she had fainted. Her mind flipped back to when she was in biology class in junior high school. She remembered that seconds before she hit the concrete floor, she had the same sickening feeling. It happened with the first slit into a motionless pithed frog, which her teacher said meant brain scrambled, lying belly up with all four stiff scrawny legs jetting straight up in the air. Rachel wasn't sure if the culprit for her temporary checkout had been from the strong nauseating odor that played havoc with her olfactory senses or if it was the first sight of the slimy guts seeping out of the belly's incision.

The next thing she remembered seeing was her teacher, Ms. Chin, and all the other students standing around her. She was disoriented at first, but soon realized she would have to resume the morbid task of mutilating the poor amphibian. To her relief, Ms. Chin told her to go directly to the first-aid room. Her teacher had asked her if she needed assistance from a fellow student. Much to the dismay of the other students, who were elbow deep inside their own frogs, she told her she would go solo.

She remembered how she staggered through the endless halls that lead to the first-aid room, which was located adjacent to the main office of Principal Phillips—alias the "prince of darkness," named by the majority of the students. He seemed to spend most of his time in his office waiting for his next victim to come in and beg for his forgiveness, which was unlikely, unless the student could pull a stellar excuse out of their ass.

More times than not, the unruly student would be condemned to mopping the cafeteria floor for a full week after school. It was one of the few times the school's grumpy janitor's mood would improve, knowing he wouldn't have to do the chore that week. And better yet, knowing he could be a dictator for a week and scrutinize every swipe of the mop.

She remembered that by the time she had arrived at the first-aid room, how the cool, moist sweat hugged her body in response to the sauna that decided to form within her. She was immediately instructed to lie down on the only horizontal structure in the room that looked to be an ancient cot sent straight from the barracks of World War II. The cot had probably been donated by some parent who tired of the guilt rope the school cast out, reminding them they needed to support the school with donations, volunteering, or better yet, both.

The reluctance for her to lie down was confirmed when she carefully felt the instability of the rickety contraption. Crashing down on to the hard and supposedly sterile floor would not have been a good thing, considering her condition. A wet cold cloth had been slapped on her forehead by the pseudo-nurse, who was probably another parent who'd succumbed to the guilt rope. Rachel was delighted she had dodged the dastardly bullet of dissecting the frog. Fainting had been worth it.

Chapter 12

Ted Parchelli was Seattle's head of homicide. Tall and gangly, he looked older than his fifty years. He was about as compassionate as a great white and had a personality as flat as cardboard. Intimidating everyone in his unit was one thing he excelled at. He was disliked by most, but respected by all. Anyone who did not respect him didn't work for him long. He did a damn good job since joining the force twenty years ago, solving more homicide cases than any of his predecessors.

Out of duty, as well as bitterness, he expected his force to have the same work ethic as he—long hours and the job placed as top priority. He had little patience or sympathy for those officers who had families and distractions. Asking for time off, including vacation time, would put the employee at the bottom of the bucket for upcoming promotions. He did this partially because he wanted his station to run as efficiently as possible, and partially out of spite. If he didn't have a happy family, then why should others enjoy family time? If he had no one to spend the holidays with, then why should they? As a result, the officers spent more time inside the four dingy walls of the station than with their own families.

Parchelli's family existed of himself and alcohol. Tipping the bottle back was the only way for him to soak up the misery he felt and was the only serum that would quiet the demons that lived within him. Without it, he would implode. There was nothing that scotch and water couldn't solve. At least not temporarily. He was a high-functioning alcoholic. No one at work knew. No one would ever know. Having earned high respect, he didn't want anything to taint his reputation. He couldn't ever jeopardize his job. His job and booze were the only two things he had left.

He had been married once and thought of his ex-wife, Glenda, often. He would never forgive himself for the mistakes he had made with her. It had been ten years since the divorce, and the regret still hit him like a wrecking ball. If only he had seen it coming, if only he had made different choices. Glenda tried everything to save the marriage—counselors, marriage seminars, books, but he didn't take any of it seriously. In his mind, all was OK. Yes, she had been complaining to him for years about how tired she was of his verbal abuse, the fighting, and his infantile temper tantrums, but he didn't think she was serious when she brought up divorce. He never thought she would leave him. He felt assured that she would put up with his abuse, his temper, and his long hours at work. She always had.

Then he was slapped in the face when he was served with divorce papers. He desperately begged her to give him another chance—he was sorry, he would change. It was too late. She didn't even give him the chance to take one bite of humble pie. It was over.

He was crumbling inside, but the armor he wore at work didn't show any cracks. He willed himself to stay stoic—show no weakness. Weakness would only compromise the respect he'd earned, and that may cause him to completely lose control, both professionally and personally.

Upon reflection, he realized he really had been an ass the entire sixteen years of the marriage. How stupid of him. She was a good woman, and he allowed her to slip right through his fingers. Women like Glenda were hard to find. He carried the bitterness with him wherever he went, and those in his path felt the ramifications.

He lived in a small house that he had owned for twenty years. It was in desperate need of a facelift—it looked as tired and worn out as he did. His intention was always to start little projects on the weekends to bring the house up to date, but somehow, those plans were always preempted by his visit to Bob's Tavern. He would rather put a drink in his hand than a paintbrush any day of the week.

Paul was the head bartender at Bob's, and he and Ted had developed a friendship throughout the years. Paul was a huge strapping man of about six-feet-six in stature and weighed close to three hundred pounds. Ted knew underneath all that muscle was a scared little rat, just like himself. Ted spent at least three nights a week sitting across from Paul on the same stool and drinking the same drink. Paul was the only person he trusted and was a great sounding board for his misery, just as he was a great sounding board for Paul's. Paul was as bitter as Ted because of how his life had turned out. He had taken his share of blows and life had certainly not been fair to him.

Paul was also divorced, many times over—four to be exact. Each marriage had produced one kid just like clockwork, ranging in age from three to fifteen. Almost every dime he made went toward child support. At the end of the month, there was little money left, so he tried to work as much overtime as possible. His gut ached every time he scratched out the four checks to the four women for the four kids he rarely saw. He never missed a payment though. Even on months when money was tight, he was somehow able to provide.

Ted and Paul were best friends, but even so, they had agreed to one rule that would not be compromised. Paul would serve Ted as many drinks as he wanted as long as he would hand over his car keys at Paul's discretion. The cabbie's phone number had been programmed into Ted's phone and he knew the taxi driver well. A DUI on Ted's record wouldn't fare well, considering his profession.

"Hi, Ted, it's Monica."

Ted had no respect for most women, but Monica was one of the exceptions. Through the years of working together, he had grown to like her and trust her. He vowed to himself to never marry again, feeling the "death do we part" vow was a crock of crap. He had experienced that the hard way. But if he ever took a chance again, it would be with someone of Monica's caliber—beautiful, intelligent, and blessed with a rockin' body—a rare combination.

"Hey, stranger! I haven't heard from you forever! How the hell are ya?" Ted's annoying voice reverberated through the phone into Monica's ear. Like most people, Monica didn't particularly like Ted either, but she smothered him with charm anyway. Ted was too valuable to lose as a cohort in solving crimes. Working with him had lined her pockets well financially.

"I'm good. Hey, I wanted to talk to you about the recent murder of Lisa Connelly. There's someone you should talk to," Monica said.

"The murderer hopefully," Ted laughed.

"No, not quite that good, but it may be the next best thing."

"That's an interesting statement, what'cha got," Ted urged.

"I met a woman a few weeks ago who had been having dreams of being murdered by the Heartbreak Killer. She was concerned that the dreams were a premonition. After meeting her, I told her that she needn't worry about getting murdered. I didn't sense any danger. But then she came to me again last week, before Lisa Connelly even went missing, saying she had a dream about the Heartbreak Killer murdering Lisa. She described the murder in great detail. Since it wasn't actually Lisa Connelly who was consulting with me, I just blew it off—didn't take it seriously. Now I wish I had."

"Hmm," he responded. "How do you know she's not the murderer, or an accomplice? You know as well as I do that half of these narcissistic, crazy whack jobs get off on all of the publicity the news creates."

"I know she's not involved because I tapped into the dream she had about Lisa. I haven't worked with you with regards to dreams, so let me explain to you how it works. When I deal with dreams, I connect with the client and experience the dream with them. In other words, I have the ability to see the dream as they see it," Monica explained.

"How do you do that?"

"We hold hands and close our eyes and my client concentrates on the dream. If they stray from their visions, the energy is lost and we must start over. It takes intense concentration from the client, as well as myself, for the energy to transfer and the knowledge to be passed. You can liken it to the way a power cord transfers electricity from a wall outlet to a computer. It's a transfer of energy. Once we are in unison, which usually takes a few minutes, I am able to see and relive the dream inside their head. I can see in my head exactly what they see in their dream. I can feel what they feel. I know this probably sounds a bit far-fetched for you—that's normal for someone who doesn't have psychic abilities."

"I see," Ted said. "I want you to know that the only person I would believe this from would be you, and that's only because you have solved so many crimes for us. So just to reiterate, when you envisioned this dream with this woman, you saw that she has no connection to the crime itself—just a vision of it."

"Exactly," Monica concurred. "She sees it as a third party. She is not directly involved in the actual crime, she's just a spectator. Therefore, she knows details about the murderer. Ted, this guy is not a typical killer. From what she tells me, and from what I've witnessed in the dreams, we've got a real twisted one on our hands here."

"Sounds juicy," Ted said skeptically, working his jaw.

Sensing Ted's hesitation, Monica said, "Ted, you know how accurate I am, right? I've never once failed you or led you astray. I'm telling you, this girl is not a fake. She knew this was going to happen."

"Hey," Ted replied apologetically. "I didn't mean to come off as not trusting you. Hell, I trust you more than I do a lot of the guys on the squad."

"Good, then I'll send her in. You need to meet with her."

"For you, my dear," Ted said, "I'll do anything."

"Oh, and Ted?" Monica said.

"Yeah?"

"Go easy on her, OK?"

The last thing Monica heard was Ted laughing in her ear before the phone went dead.

Rachel's appointment with Ted Parchelli at the police station was set for nine o'clock that morning and she was running late. There had been an accident on the freeway and traffic was backed up for miles. When she finally got to the station, she swung into a parking space at breakneck speed. She took the stairs two at a time instead of waiting for the elevator.

When Rachel finally rushed in, she told the woman sitting at the front desk who she was. The woman appeared to be in her late fifties with shoulder-length gray perma-hair. Apparently, she had seen the bad half of society for too many years. Her worn-out face had no sympathy for Rachel's tardiness. "You're late, take a seat. I'll tell him you're here," she growled. Perma-Hair sighed as she picked up the phone to summon Ted as if it were an insurmountable task. "Ted, your nine o'clock is here."

Rachel heard the man's strange gait before she spotted his face. He came at her with an angry expression. "Ms. Carter," he snapped.

"Yes, hi," Rachel responded, stood up, and held out her hand to greet him, "Sorry, I'm late, I—"

"Glad you could make it," he responded sarcastically, cutting her off and keeping his hand to himself.

"I'm so sorry, I . . . I . . ."

"Save it, we don't have time for excuses, and our sketch artist doesn't have all day to wait," Ted said harshly, looming over her. Rachel just nodded, guilty as charged. *I'm certainly glad I don't work for this jerk, or her,* she thought, giving perma-hair a furtive look.

She followed Ted and his long legs down the hall, focusing on his bald head as it bobbed up and down with his authoritative walk. He led her down the hall to his office. It was larger than the other offices she had passed, but not by much. When they reached his office, he walked around his heavy metal desk and sat down and motioned for her to do the same in the chair opposite him. The chair, which was also metal, had a torn brown cushion that sprouted out a plume of foam. It looked like it had been sat in a thousand times before, probably by a thousand guilty criminals. The whole place gave her the willies, and she was beginning to wish that Monica had not sent her to see Ted Parchelli.

Ted flipped open a file in front of him and started reading it intently, ignoring her. She could finally get a good look at him. Usual police attire, average looking. Thin, blue eyes, thin lips, thick black-framed glasses, clean shaven, bald, and well over six feet. After she had scoped him out, she glanced around his office. Hundreds of files—some thick, some thin. An antiquated computer with a worn-down keyboard sat on his desk, "attaboy" plaques hung on the wall behind him. There were no family pictures or signs of a personal life at all. *That figures,* Rachel thought. *He didn't come across as a family man. How could anyone in their right mind stand him?*

Ted tossed the open file across the desk to Rachel and pictures of Lisa's dead body slipped halfway out. Rachel sucked in air, covered her mouth, and looked up at him with a terrified expression.

"Ms. Carter, it shouldn't be so offensive or surprising to you. That's what you saw, wasn't it—in your dream?"

"Yes, b-but . . . ," Rachel stammered. She was speechless.

"But what? Weren't you expecting to see the real thing? Well there it is," he said, pointing to the photos.

"Yeah, well, it's a little different when you see it in a real photograph!" Rachel exclaimed.

"Look, Ms. Carter. The only reason I am even talking to you about Ms. Connelly is because Monica Rupert gave me a call and told me that you had some dreams about Ms. Connelly's death prior to it. Now, normally, I wouldn't waste my time, but because I trust Monica, I am willing to check out this whole matter," he said, staring her down with beady eyes that were placed too close together.

Rachel was furious. "Look, Mr. Parchelli, you are not doing me any favors here. I am the one helping you! If you don't want information from me, then I am more than happy to leave. In fact, I would rather leave than deal with your rudeness. Evidently, there's been a misunderstanding on my part. The only reason *I'm here* talking to *you* about this is because Monica asked *me* to come in with the idea that I could perhaps be of some help." She took in a big breath and waited.

Ted was taken aback at Rachel's change in attitude and her blossoming confidence. He liked strong women, and she was definitely one. She'd earned his respect.

"Understood. Then let's do this. Let's work on catching this bastard together," he said, his voice deathly even.

Rachel was surprised at how quickly Ted was disarmed. "Fair enough," she huffed. Rachel and Ted spent the next two hours talking about Rachel's dream of Lisa Connelly, as well as the dream she was having about her own murder.

Once they were done talking, Ted led her into a small room where an absolutely gorgeous man sat behind a desk, staring at his computer screen. She felt her heart flutter and suddenly quicken when he looked up.

"Brett," Ted commanded. "This is Ms. Carter. Ms. Carter, this is Brett, our sketch artist." It was apparent from both sides that when Brett and Rachel exchanged looks, there was a magnetic pull. She stood there stunned for a second longer than she should have before responding, baffled at what to say.

Thankfully, Brett broke the silence, relieving her of how awkward she must've appeared. "Please, have a seat," he said in a southern accent. She did so without a word and placed her purse gently on the floor beside her.

"So I hear we need to put a face on a killer," Brett said, clasping his hands together on top of his desk, his beautiful eyes looking intently into hers. The faint smell of cinnamon seeped from his breath—her favorite scent.

Rachel tried to be subtle about the physical attraction she was feeling. She felt like a schoolgirl being face to face with her first crush. The thick, cropped salt-and-pepper hair; the chiseled features; the captivating gray eyes. He was wearing a dark blue short-sleeved shirt, exposing his tanned muscular arms. The most important attraction, however, was that he wasn't wearing a wedding ring.

True, every married man doesn't wear a wedding ring. Maybe he fell into that category. On the other hand, it may not be as good as it appears. If not married, Rachel was sure he had already been scooped up by some beautiful woman. But she didn't see any pictures of a woman on his desk. *That's a good thing.* But if he wasn't attached already, she was sure he had numerous women chasing after him, being as handsome and polite as he was. *Not to mention the sexy accent.*

"Yes," Rachel croaked, her voice as dry as sandpaper.

"Fantastic, let's get started," Brett said, pushing aside his computer, which was just as old and outdated as Parchelli's. He bent down to grab something out of the lower drawer of his desk—enabling Rachel enough time to ogle him without being discovered. *Wow.* Although she couldn't tell how tall he was from a sitting position, she surmised he was well within the range of what she looked for in a man's height. He sat up and placed a large sketch pad, a few sharpened pencils, and a huge eraser on his desk.

"OK, here we go . . . ," he said, holding his pencil down on the sketch pad. He was a lefty—just like her. *Common ground . . . another good thing,* she thought. "Let's start with the shape of his face. Round? Square? Long?" he asked, looking up at her. Rachel studied Brett's face—God, he was devilishly handsome.

"Hmm," she paused, placing her pointer finger under her chin in deep thought. "I have to think about that for a second because what I was mainly drawn to was a large scar on the left side of his face."

"Good . . . that little fact will help us distinguish him easier. Those are the kinds of details that are very important in putting this sketch together. Take your time to think, Rachel, about every detail—no matter how subtle you may think it is. A small detail could prove to be very important in identifying the murderer."

Rachel took a few more minutes to think, her eyes focused up toward the ceiling. A few seconds went by as she sat there in quiet deliberation. "I would say his face is more broad—square like. It's not round or oval," she said, casting her eyes back down.

"Perfect," Brett said with a pleasing look on his face. Slowly, he began to lightly sketch on the pad. After a moment, Brett slid the sketch over to Rachel, "Would you say this is pretty close to the shape of his face?"

"From what I remember, yes," she said, sliding the sketch back to him.

"Good," he encouraged her to proceed. Once again, he picked up his pencil. "Let's focus on his eyes. This is a very important area since many people are recognized just by their eyes. Do you remember the shape? Were they close together? Far apart? Big? Small?" he asked, cocking his head in an adorable expression.

"I would say they were large, with a roundish shape. He had a few creases at the edges," she said, displaying outstretched fingers at the outer part of her eyes indicating crow's feet. "He looked like he was maybe in his mid-thirties. I don't remember his eyes being spread far apart or really close. I would say they were just a normal distance from each other."

Brett concentrated as he drew the eyes, trying to replicate the description Rachel had given him. "Did he have real visible eyelids? Less visible? Invisible eyes lids?" he asked, keeping his head down, looking at the pair of eyes he had just drawn.

"Normal, I would say," Rachel answered immediately.

"OK," he took a deep breath. "Let's talk about color. Were you close enough to see the color of his eyes?"

"Yes," she replied. "During Lisa's murder, he turned on the light and I was able to get fairly close to him. He had brown eyes—dark brown."

He filled in the irises with his pencil and scribbled a note on the side, depicting the color.

Rachel was amazed out how accurate Brett's sketch was. "Wow," she said, expressing surprise, "I thought it would take longer to get it right—so far, it's perfect."

Brett just smiled. "Eyebrows—Bushy? Thin? Curved normal? Curved strange?"

"I remember they were bushy—in fact, they were very bushy, but normally shaped, not like a unibrow or anything," she said. Both Brett and Rachel chuckled. Brett sketched them quickly.

"What about his nose?"

"It was long, but broad," she said, tracing an invisible line down her nose with her finger. Rachel watched as Brett sketched the killer's nose.

"Is that about right?" Brett asked after he completed the nose.

"Yes, exactly!" Rachel said. "Wow, you are so good at this."

"Moving on to the mouth," he continued. "Large? Small? Full lips? Thin lips?"

She paused to think. "Um, his lips were kind of large—thick."

"The plump type of lips that most men like on a woman?" he asked, winking at Rachel. She knew he was probably joking, but also thought that plump lips must be a feature that he likes in a woman, or he wouldn't have mentioned it. She thought about her own lips and subconsciously ran a finger across them—definitely not plump. *Strike one.*

Brett again turned the sketch toward Rachel. She studied the mouth, mainly the lips, very closely. She noticed for the first time he got the look wrong. "No," she said. "The shape is off."

"OK, does the mouth curve more downward? Upward? Straight? Is it proportional with the face? Too large. Too small?"

"Well," Rachel bit her lip as she studied the sketch closely. "I don't know. I mean I remember seeing it, but to be honest, I didn't spend a lot of time looking at his mouth."

"I can understand why that would be, considering there was a lot going on." He frowned, shaking his head. "These murderers . . . I don't know how they can do it." He turned around and reached for a large black binder lying on the credenza behind his desk.

"Let's see," he said, opening the binder to where it was labeled "Mouths." "Maybe this will help," Brett said, angling the book toward her. She reached for it and looked at the first example. It couldn't have been more different than the killer's. She spent several minutes slowly turning the plastic-covered pages, looking at the variety of mouths. She was amazed at how many mouth types there were. "That's it," she said, putting her index finger on the sketch that illustrated the killer's mouth the closest.

"Ahh, that was the problem," he explained. "The bow of the top lip is quite pronounced."

"Yes, I had forgotten that, but there it is," she told him confidently, nodding her head.

"That's why we have the book," he said, smiling and closing it. He placed the book aside. He erased the mouth he had drawn, revised it, and then passed it back to Rachel. She was astonished at how his drawing was a perfect replica of the one in the notebook as well as that of the killer's.

"Perfect . . . you are amazing. How long have you been doing this?"

He looked up at her with a sly expression. "Let's just say a long time." Although he didn't reveal his age, Rachel thought he looked to be in his late thirties, early forties. She surmised he had his shit together, unlike most of the men she had dated close to her own age.

"Teeth?" he asked.

"Pretty straight." Brett jotted down "straight teeth" on one side of the pad.

"Cheekbones? High? Low? Average?"

"I didn't notice that, so they must've been normal."

"Hair?"

"Most of it was covered because he wore a black knit cap. But there was some hair at the fringe that was visible—wavy and dark brown."

"Ears?" Brett asked.

"Again, mostly covered, but the bottoms appeared normal."

"Now, on to that scar you mentioned . . . ," he said.

"It was on the left side of his face. It was deep, very visible. It extended from under his left eyebrow down to the top of his lip—slanted," she explained, using her finger to draw an imaginary scar on her face. Brett carefully drew the scar onto the face he had just constructed.

"For the record, other than the face, what about his physique—large? Small? Heavy? Slight? Tall? Short?"

"Definitely very tall—well over six feet, not thin, not fat—just huge," Rachel explained, spreading her arms out to her sides. Brett made some notes on the side of the sketch and then handed the pad to Rachel. Rachel was absolutely stunned at his accuracy. "My god, Brett, you are dead on."

"That's my goal," he said with a crooked smile and winked at her.

Chapter 13

Rachel sat across from Heather at Joe's. A tune from Elvis Presley was streaming through the speakers. The wicked waitress wasn't there this time. Considering how rude she was, Rachel hoped she'd been fired. Certain people are just not meant to interact with public, and that woman was one. Perma-hair was another. They belonged behind a desk somewhere with absolutely no personal interaction.

"Wasn't that eerie that I had a dream about her murder?" Rachel asked warily.

"Oh my god, that is very scary! Now there's no question as to your psychic abilities—I just can't believe it. I hope now Monica is taking you a little more seriously," Heather said with disgust. "I'm glad you went to her, but she should have listened to you when you first told her about your dream. Lisa may still be alive."

"No kidding," Rachel's face tightened and her jaw clenched.

"And you are still having the dreams about yourself?"

"Yes. That's what is so unnerving."

"Hopefully they'll catch this wacko before anyone else ends of dead," Heather said.

"You mean catch him before *I* end up dead?"

"Well, I didn't really mean it that way," Heather recoiled.

"Yes, you did," Rachel said, attempting to stay calm.

Heather shrugged her shoulders. "What can I say, Rachel? I just hope they catch him soon. Now that the police know you are for real and not a fake, hopefully they'll start taking your premonitions seriously. The police need to do something to protect you from this psychopath."

"I don't think they're going to do that," Rachel responded. "Especially because Monica still doesn't think I, myself, am in danger. The important thing is they keep focused on finding him before he gets too close. I hate having to look over my shoulder all the time."

"What? Monica *still* doesn't think you're in danger?"

"Well, she says that she would've known if I was in danger when she connected with me. She says the dreams I'm having about my own murder are just nightmares," Rachel said, tensing her shoulders. "I'm not convinced."

"How does she know you're not in danger? I mean, you were right about Lisa."

"She says she would've gotten a *feeling* or some bullshit if I was actually in danger. She says she can tell the difference between a premonition and a nightmare," Rachel said, rolling her eyes.

"And she didn't get any indication you were in danger? She told you it was just a nightmare?"

"According to her, that's right."

"I don't know . . . that whole *connection* thing seems weird to me."

"It was weird. I couldn't believe she could actually relive the dream with me. It sent shivers down my spine."

"The good thing is . . . is that Monica is very well known for her accuracy, so if she doesn't think you're in danger, she's probably right. That should calm your nerves to some extent."

"It doesn't. Not at all. They need to find this guy soon," Rachel said, a storm visibly started to brew on her face.

"That's for sure," Heather exhaled hard. "Just don't be telling me if *I'm* the one who shows up in your dreams."

"Are you kidding me? I'd tell you right away."

"I'd rather not know. Ignorance is bliss sometimes."

"Not in this situation," Rachel said. "But don't worry. I haven't had any dreams about you getting murdered."

"I hope you don't," Heather said.

"The good news is that I met with the sketch artist yesterday. I was able to give him a description of the killer I saw in my dream."

"Was the sketch artist pretty good?" Heather inquired.

"Yes, in more ways than one," Rachel smiled.

"What's that mean?"

"He's gorgeous. My perfect-looking guy," Rachel gushed and licked her lips.

"*Really*," Heather responded seductively.

"Yes. His name is Brett. He's about six feet tall, nice build, gray short hair, gorgeous gray eyes, killer smile—and talk about sweet—oh my gosh. He has the whole package," Rachel purred.

"Well then, you will have to put on some of that Rachel charm we both know so well."

"It's kind of weird to concentrate on my charm when he is sketching the lunatic who is plotting to slaughter me. But I will tell you that if the killer gets caught and I'm still breathing, Brett won't have a chance. I'll entice him with my full charm."

"Why wait? Maybe he can be around to protect you now," Heather suggested.

"I don't need a man to protect me," Rachel argued.

"We all need a man for something, Rachel," Heather said, rolling her eyes.

"That, I will agree with," Rachel said, pursing her lips into a tight smile. "I could use a handyman around every once in a while. I can barely hang a picture by myself." Just then, another thought bloomed within her mind. "What if he has a girlfriend, or a wife and kids?"

"Girlfriend? That shouldn't stop you," Heather said, curling her lip up in a wicked smile.

"I know," Rachel said, beaming and bubbling over with excitement. "Now if he has a wife . . . that's a different story."

It was dangerous though. It was almost as if Brett were giving her some false sense of security by merely sketching the killer.

She found herself thinking of Brett as she walked to her car. The pleasant thoughts soon faded as she noticed that some idiot had parked so close to the driver side of her car that there was no way she was going to squeeze in. She would have to enter from the passenger side and crawl into the driver seat. She felt her blood boil as she squirmed her way over the awkward console.

"Son of a bitch!" she said out loud as she finally plopped down in the driver seat, her backside hurting from being jabbed by the hand brake. She was fuming. She screeched out of the parking spot, stopped, grabbed a cup of old coffee that had been sitting in her cup holder for days, rolled down her window, and threw the cup at the car. She watched it bounce off the windshield and land on the icy pavement. Her mission to douse the car with cold coffee had been accomplished. "Maybe you'll think about someone other than yourself the next time you park your damn car!" A thought raced through Rachel's head that if the parking lot had security cameras, she may very well end up in jail. *Probably the safest place for me to be, unless the nutcase can penetrate steel bars.*

Chapter 14

His mother's voice reverberated in his head.

'She's the one.'

He looked up at his mother's picture with her wry smile and viscous black eyes.

'You need to kill her for me—look how cute she is. She will blossom into a beauty soon, so she must die now.'

"But, Mother, she is too young. She is much younger than the others, she . . ." He wished he had never thought of the girl while his mother watched him. She could read his mind when he was this close to her. She knew his thoughts. She saw what images were in his head.

'Randall, remember you are not the one who makes the decision on who dies and who lives,' his mother's voice said, escalating. He knew better than to question her again. He had tried before, and there was no reasoning with her. "OK, Mother—OK," he uttered, closing his eyes tightly,

clenching his fist to conceal his anger, his mouth growing into a tight line.

Danielle Perkins was a pretty and popular cheerleader at Pioneer High School. She was only a smidge over five feet tall, had long black straight hair, and big brown eyes that earned her the nickname "Bambi."

Her smile monopolized much of her face and it reflected her spunky, vibrant personality well. She had been captain of the cheer squad for two years now and hung with the popular crowd. She was loved by all, including the girls who would normally be jealous of a person like her. The reason being is that she was nice to everybody—not just the popular kids. She made time to talk to everyone, regardless of their social status within the school. In her eyes, they were all equal.

She was different from the other popular kids. She decided to deviate from the normal arrogance of the so-called privileged crowd. Being the type of person that she was, she would always take outcasts under her wing. If someone was eating alone at lunch, her heart would break for them. She would often pick up her tray and go join them. Those that she took in, like a savior, loved her dearly for caring about them. Her compassion and kindness reached far beyond the capability of the normal egocentric teenager. When she "saved" the outcasts, her group of friends didn't question her kindness. They knew that Danielle was . . . well . . . she was just being Danielle.

She set up and coordinated after-school programs such as feeding the homeless and donating the little extra time she had to being a big sister to girls who were placed in foster care. Although students were reluctant to participate at first and join her in helping, many were now following in her quest to work with the less privileged. Danielle was one in a million. That was for sure—something everyone recognized.

Randall had spotted her on the news when the station showed a clip on the success her high school's football team was having that season. The reporter had interviewed the coach, a few football players, and Danielle after a major victory last week. Danielle caught Randall's eye. She was absolutely adorable.

Was she dreaming? Rachel was trapped again, unable to move. She was floating above a parking lot when she suddenly saw the murderer . . .

Randall knew what car Danielle drove, and he knew exactly where she would park it. He stood waiting in the shadows. He welcomed the cold, earthy, smell of pine that spilled from the trees.

He knew that because Danielle was a cheerleader, she would be there well before the football game started. And she was. The Mini Cooper pulled into the lot at breakneck speed. Danielle screeched into her usual spot.

"Don't you dare touch that girl. That's all she is—a young girl!" Rachel yelled. Her panic escalated, but her vocal chords failed her.

Danielle was so cute. He couldn't really use the word "beautiful" yet because she was so young. He watched her as she hopped out of her car, wearing her black and red cheerleading uniform. The top was white and red; and the short, little, pleated wool skirt was black. He saw her reach back into the car to grab her pom-poms—huge fluffy balls of red and white. The game was to start exactly at seven. Randall had been hiding out since six to make sure he was there when she pulled in.

"So help me, God. If you hurt her, may you burn in hell!" Rachel screamed her silent rage as she looked down at him.

Randall heard the cheers and yells of the cheerleaders during the football game and wondered which one was Danielle's. They were always yelling in unison about how great their team was and how bad the other team was. He couldn't see her from his hiding spot, but he could imagine how cute she would look leading the cheer. But he couldn't think about that now. Randall needed to get to her car. It was during the second quarter when he made his first move. He wanted the parking lot vacant when he did so. He needed to make it quick.

He cautiously made his way to her car and took out the small wire cutters he carried with him. Lifting the hood just a foot or so, he used his flashlight to locate and cut the wires to disable the car. Just a few snips and he was done. Randall shut the hood quietly and walked cautiously back to his hiding spot, looking around to make sure no one was watching him.

Rachel watched him in disgust. "You son of a bitch. How can you butcher such an innocent girl?"

He squatted down and listened to the rest of the game, the cheering crowds, and all the other sounds that resonate from football games. He had never been into football. As a small child, his parents encouraged him to try out for the team, but he didn't have the competitive spirit for it. Sure his size would give him an advantage, but he wouldn't have been able to hurt a fly.

After the game ended, Danielle started to walk to her car. Their team had won, and she was glad to be on her way home. She loved to cheer, but when it was this cold, she wondered if it was all worth it. Her legs felt like they were made of solid icicles as she moved quickly across the parking lot. She had never felt safe walking alone at night. Yes, there were other people heading to their cars; but she was small, and it wouldn't take much for someone to snatch her without anyone seeing. For some reason, she felt more vulnerable than usual. She felt a shudder slink down her spine but she didn't know why.

Randall watched as Danielle approached her car. The other cars in the parking lot were leaving or had already left. She was looking around and Randall figured it was out of being cautious. It didn't matter, he thought. No amount of cautiousness on her part could keep her from him.

She unlocked the car door and worked her way into the driver's seat. Using her keys, she tried to start the car, but it wouldn't start. She continued for a good five minutes to no avail. Randall was relieved; he had hoped he had cut the correct wires. When Danielle was the only one left in the lot, Randall made his approach. He made sure she didn't see him. Randall was cloaked in all black and he blended into the darkness, but still he had to be careful. He didn't want her to get out of the car and start running. He had seen her run before and she was quick. He was very close now and didn't want her to escape.

"Be careful, he's coming! Lock your doors," Rachel screeched from her perch as Randall approached the car.

"Lock your doors!" Rachel cried again. Then her focus shifted to Randall. She read what was going through his mind. She mirrored his thoughts, his emotions, and his remorse, just as in the other murders. He didn't want to do this. Out of all the murders he had committed, this one bothered him the most.

She was too young to die. Why did his mother have to choose someone so young? He would certainly find no satisfaction or joy from killing her. What he felt was immense grief. But the repercussions he would be subjected to if he didn't follow through with his mother's demand overshadowed any amount of grief he felt.

"C'mon, don't do this! You know in your own mind how wrong this is! Your mother is dead, dead! She is not telling you to do this. It's all in your mind!" Rachel thought, hoping to penetrate his mind.

Nothing. Again.

It was just as before—she could read his mind, but he couldn't read hers.

Crouching, he was now directly behind her car. He was in the clear. There was just enough illumination in the parking lot from the field lights for him to see her reflection in the side mirror. Danielle was on her cell phone, probably calling someone to explain her dilemma and hoping to hitch a ride. He needed to move fast.

"He's right there!" Rachel cried out. "Lock your door! Hurry!"

Once she was off the phone, he pounced like a lion would onto a lamb. He was glad she had been careless enough to leave the door unlocked. But he was prepared for it if she had locked her door because he carried a crowbar that he could use to break the window.

She jumped when he opened the door. He saw the look of terror spread across her face. Dammit, he didn't want to look into her face. He could kill her, but not while looking at her. He didn't want to see her fear. She lurched back into the passenger side of the car, kicking and screaming violently. He reached into the car to cover her mouth.

"That's it, keep kicking, keep fighting. Kick the son of a bitch on his ass!" Rachel screamed.

She put up a good fight, but Randall was able to overpower her in the cramped space and quickly covered her mouth with some duct tape he had been carrying to stifle her cries. He usually didn't need to add duct tape to his regimen, but the high school wasn't as remote as the other places he had captured his victims at, and he needed her quiet. Her muffled cries broke his heart. Desperate cries always broke his heart. Why couldn't they make it easier for him and just not cry? He pulled her out of the car.

"Oh god," Rachel said in a voice of defeat. "He's got you now honey, he's got you now."

He carried her back into the bushes beyond where he had been hiding out, gently placed her on the ground, and straddled her. She was flailing like a captured animal in the grip of its predator. Avoiding her arms, he flipped her over. Randall was surprised at how strong Danielle was in spite of her pint-size.

Once he secured her, he reached into the death pack for the knife—the one object that transformed him from the man he truly was into the beast his mother had forced him to become.

He sat there on top of Danielle until she fatigued from her struggle. He wanted to make sure she heard what he had to say.

Rachel was finally able to float down beside them. She tried to reach out to grab the knife, but just as before, she was paralyzed. She spoke into his ear. "Please, listen to me. You can't kill this one. Look at her, she's just a baby, can't you see that?"

"Danielle," he bent down and softly whispered in her ear. "I want you to know that out of all the girls I've taken, you will be the hardest to kill. Please forgive me."

With that, Danielle tried to scream and struggled violently. He couldn't understand her words because of the duct tape, but he didn't need to. "Danielle, you must be quiet, or I will have to make this harder for you." With that, her cries quieted a bit. "You see, I didn't want to think about you in front of my mother, but I did. She knows all of my thoughts, and when I thought of you, she saw how cute you were and how beautiful you would become. Now she wants you dead. I tried to talk her out of it. I told her I would find someone else to kill, but she wouldn't listen to me. She never does. She only gets angry if I argue with her. But for you, I pleaded with her. I asked her to spare you." He hoped his words would somehow comfort her—make her feel special.

Danielle turned her head to the side in an effort to look at him—reason with him somehow. She felt the freezing ground penetrate through her. Even through her gloves, her fingers had become numb from clawing at shards of snow and ice in her effort to break free.

He grabbed her head with his hand and turned it back toward the frozen ground. She fought against him, but the pressure he was putting on her was too strong for her to resist. With the other hand he placed the knife below one ear.

"God . . . oh my god!" Rachel shouted, her panic escalating as tears burned behind her eyes.

"Shhh . . . shhh . . . it will be quick . . . I promise. I'll make sure of that. I won't leave you, I promise. I will be here the whole time. Some people in this world end up dying alone. But you won't be one of them, Danielle. I'm here for you," Randall said in his attempt to console her. He eased the pressure from the hand that was holding her head down and started to stroke her hair. "You have such beautiful hair—so innocent," he said. Then he grabbed a handful of it and pulled it back, exposing her neck. She was too innocent to die, and at that moment, he hated his mother. He saw plumes of frost coming out of her sweet nose with every panicked breath she took. How sad it was to know that that would soon stop, along with everything else.

"Please forgive me, Danielle," he whispered. Without another thought, he sliced her.

Rachel watched Randall cover Danielle's body with snow and frozen leaves in a shallow grave. He left her just like the others—her head barely attached to her body.

Rachel woke suddenly with one big gasp and sat straight up in bed. Danielle, whoever she was, was next.

Shaking uncontrollably, she reached to turn the light on, knocking a full glass of water over onto the floor. Cali bolted from the room. Rachel's bed sheets were twisted around her like an out-of-control vine and she had to fight to free herself. She opened her nightstand drawer and frantically searched for the anxiety pills her doctor had mindlessly prescribed to her after spending a mere two minutes with her in the exam room.

Finally, she found the pills and grabbed them with a shaking hand. She was trembling so bad that she dropped them; they hit the floor and rolled. She tried to move, but even as she unraveled the sheets around her, her body felt as if it were buried in cement. She was afraid to even walk. Finally, she moved. She picked up the pill bottle off the floor, opened it, put three pills in her mouth, and swallowed them dry. It was over the dosage, but at that point, she didn't care.

She staggered to the kitchen to call Monica. "Dammit," she cursed to herself. *Where was Monica's business card?* After shoving the papers and letters aside that were occupying the counter, she finally spotted the card beside the coffee pot. She scooped it up and picked up the phone. Her head was swimming, her vision fading in and out, her ears ringing. Was she going to faint or was she just starting to hyperventilate? She could've gone ahead and called Ted Parchelli, but she felt more comfortable talking to Monica first. Especially in the state of mind she was in.

Monica's voice mail finally clicked on after too many rings. "Hello, this is Monica . . ."

Rachel panted into the phone, "Monica, oh god, Monica, please . . . please call me. He's going to kill another one. Her name is Danielle . . ." Her voice cracked. "Please, please call me before it's too late." Breathless, she slammed the phone down.

There was no way she was going back into that bedroom. She would not sleep, she would not. Staying awake was only a short comfort, but it was the only choice. Falling back asleep was not an option.

When was this psycho going to be after *her*? Today? Tomorrow? A month from now? She didn't know. She found herself looking over her shoulder every few minutes, regardless of where she was. Extra locks had been installed on her doors and windows. It still wasn't enough. She even had a security system installed, which covered all the doors and windows, and came equipped with a motion detector. Regardless of all the protection, she still felt vulnerable—awake many nights now till the break of dawn. She kept her mace and a baseball bat right next to her bed. She found herself in constant fear. Her life was hanging in the balance, her death being plotted by a maniacal serial killer.

Rachel jumped when the phone rang. "Hi, Rachel, Monica here. You dreamed about another one?"

"Yes, and this one is just a young girl—high school age. Her name is Danielle. She's a cheerleader, but I don't know at what high school. All

I know is that the school colors are red and black—that was the color of her uniform."

"Dear god. Here we go again," Monica said somberly. "Have you called Parchelli?

"No . . . should I call him or do you want to?"

"I think it would be best if you call him since you had the dream and would have more details. I think he takes you serious enough now that you can have a direct dialogue with him without my assistance."

"I'll call him right away then. The police can probably figure out which school she belongs to by the black and red colors, and I know her name is Danielle."

"Call him now! Keep me in the loop."

"OK, what's his number?"

After Monica gave her the number, she disconnected from her and immediately called Ted. She was thankful that he picked up on the second ring.

"Ted, it's Rachel. There's going to be another one."

"Give me all the details. We'll need to get on this right away."

"I know her name is Danielle and she's a high school student." Rachel's words spilled out so quickly that Ted couldn't make out what she was saying.

"Slow down, Rachel, I can't understand you."

Rachel paused and took a deep breath. "All I know is that her name is Danielle and she's a high school cheerleader. Her uniform was black and red, so I'm assuming those are the school colors."

"OK, let me get on it. Was it the same killer?" Ted asked.

"Yes, it's the Heartbreak Killer."

"I'll get right on this. I'll let you know what we find out," Ted said. "And, Rachel?"

"Yeah?"

"Thank you."

Chapter 15

Derek Johnson had taken the same trek for the past ten years with his chocolate lab, Henry. Just like every other day, he walked through the trail back behind the high school. The path was a shortcut to his house, a half a mile away. Ironically, the path was peaceful and quiet, considering it was just about thirty yards from the high school.

When Henry was a puppy, Derek had him leashed because he was a ball of fire wanting to go every which way, but now Henry knew the drill and meandered through the trail unleashed—too old and tired to roam far from his master.

Up ahead, Henry stopped to sniff the ground and began to whine and wag his tail swiftly. "Aw, old fella', what did you find up there?" Derek could see a mound of color up ahead, which didn't make sense when he first spotted it. As he got closer, his heart stopped.

"Dear god," he whispered. He finally stood and walked up closer to Danielle's body. She was partially covered by fresh snow and leaves, and he knew right away that the uniformed girl, obviously a cheerleader, was dead—lying on her stomach, facedown. Blood was everywhere. It was hard to distinguish between what was her blood and what was the material of the red sweater she had on. He didn't walk any closer. One, because he knew from all the crime shows he had watched on TV how important it was not to contaminate a crime scene; and two, he didn't really want to see any more details other than the horror of what he was already looking at.

Blended in with the blood, he saw the red wooden particle cupped in her hands above her head. It was mostly covered with fresh snowfall, which made it hard at first to determine exactly what it was. "Dear god, little girl, what happened to you?" he whispered as if he didn't know, but being up to date on the news, he already knew.

Rachel sat in front of the flat screen television set that she had splurged on last weekend with money she didn't have. Considering she was technically challenged and had no man to help her, it took her twice as long as it should've to get it set up and functioning correctly. "It sure would be nice to have a man around," she had muttered in frustration, trying to get the damn thing to work properly.

She curled up on her couch in her favorite comfy tattered plaid pajamas that she'd worn for years. They were ripped in the back, but for some reason, she couldn't bring herself to throw them out. Drac immediately jumped up on her lap to wait for his morning loving. "Hey, bud," she said, petting him in his favorite spot under his chin. He looked up at her with his adoring green eyes and his ever-present bucked fangs.

She went to pick up the television remote controller where it was supposed to be, but of course, it was missing. "OK, Drac, you gotta get down, we're missing the remote again. She stood up and started to dig underneath the pillows of the couch. After several minutes, and several sighs, she found it, pulled it out, immediately assumed her position again and clicked on the TV.

Flipping through the channels, she settled on the morning news. The forecast for the next five days was light snow and frigid temperatures. When was it going to let up? In all the years she had lived in Seattle, she had never experienced such an early winter. Rachel wasn't a big fan of rain, but it would have been a welcome change. She was getting sick and tired of trudging through snow and scraping ice off her windshield at the crack of dawn.

"Back to you, Greg," the weatherman said.

"Thanks, Jeremy. The body of Danielle Perkins, who was last seen cheering at a Pioneer High School football game last Friday, was found last night. A man walking his dog near the high school discovered her body just yards from the high school bleachers. An autopsy is scheduled to be performed, but police are suspecting foul play. There will be a vigil for Danielle this coming Wednesday night at six-thirty at the Pioneer High School football field."

Rachel put her coffee down and dropped her head into her hands. It startled her this time, but it wasn't a shock. The shock was becoming less and less with each passing murder. The police hadn't moved fast enough. "I'm sorry, Danielle. I wish we could have stopped him," Rachel murmured.

"Have you seen the news about Danielle?" Ted asked Monica anxiously through the phone line.

"Yes, I saw it today," Monica responded, rubbing her temples.

"How well do you know Rachel?"

"Why?" Monica asked curiously.

"Look, Monica, I know you told me that you don't suspect her, but I am beginning to wonder about this woman and her involvement. I just have a gut feeling that she may not be telling us everything. She just knows too much. She knew every detail about Lisa's murder, and now Danielle?"

"Ted, I can assure you that she has nothing to do with the murders other than her prediction of them. At least she didn't have any involvement with the murder of Lisa. I would have known if she was involved when I connected with her in the dream. She's innocent. I can assure you of that," Monica said confidently.

"Are you *absolutely* sure? I'm considering bringing her in for questioning."

"Ted, I am positive that she's not in any way involved. I definitely would *not* let her know that you suspect her and would *not* bring her in for questioning. It would be counterproductive. She'll just clam up if she has any more dreams about future murders. We need her to keep talking so we can nail this crazy assed killer."

"OK, I'll trust you on this one, just as I always have. But you let me know *immediately* if she tells you that she's having any more dreams," Ted said, grazing his hand over his bald head.

"Will do. Don't worry, Ted. I would know if she were in any way involved with the murders," Monica assured him and hung up.

The phone rang and Rachel jumped. She knew without a doubt who it was. "Have you heard the news?" Monica asked.

"Yes." Rachel sighed. "They found Danielle. I was really hoping my intuition on this one was wrong, but it wasn't. I spoke to Parchelli right after I talked with you about the dream, and he said he'd get right on it. But I think the killer may have already killed her or was on the verge of it when I had the dream," Rachel said, giving Ted the benefit of the doubt.

"Well, it's unfortunate. Because now, another girl is dead," Monica said, reaching around to massage her neck.

"This so-called psychic gift I have doesn't seem to be doing much good because women are still dying."

"Don't beat yourself up, Rachel. You may be psychic, but you're not a miracle worker."

At that point even Monica was tempted to tell Rachel about Parchelli's suspicions but decided not to. It would only harm the investigation. She didn't want anyone scaring Rachel off—not if it meant catching this freak.

Chapter 16

Rachel had been preparing for teacher conferences all week. These meetings were always a balancing act for Rachel. It was important to be honest with the parents about their child's level of intellect as well as their social behavior, but it was also important to communicate things in a positive way. She needed to be direct, but sensitive. It was always a challenge to decide just how much finesse she needed to use because all parents reacted differently.

If she communicated to the parents with what may seem to be the wrong words or gestures, one of three things would happen. One, the child may be disciplined in a positive way. Two, the child may be reprimanded in a negative way and in turn destroy the child's confidence. Or worst of all, they would blame Rachel for her inaccuracy and tell her how dare she label their child anything short of perfect. In the third situation, no one wins. Rachel had dealt with enough parents to experience all three scenarios.

Talking to Billy Cooper's parents was going to be a loose cannon. There were things about Billy she was obligated to say as his teacher, but she hadn't yet met his parents to know how they would react. One thing she knew for sure—if anyone needed a good swift kick in the ass, it was Billy. She would love to be the one to carry out the punishment, but for obvious reasons, she would be deprived of such a pleasure.

Rachel had always chosen to start with the hardest problem first then ease down to the easy stuff. It had always served her best to get the worst behind her initially. Billy's parents were first on her schedule. The appointment was in just a few moments, and Rachel's mind was flipping through the images of Billy's tyranny like another bad dream. How was she going to tell them that Billy was basically the devil incarnate?

If Billy continued the way he was, Rachel could see his future turning out in one of two ways—possibly both. Either he would end up viewing his world through steel bars—which may be the best thing, in Rachel's opinion, so he couldn't continue tormenting everyone in his path—or he would end up dead. Rachel had tirelessly been sending progress reports and e-mails to Billy's parents regarding his issues but hadn't received any response and last year, they didn't come to any of the student/teacher conferences.

Rachel wondered what sin she had committed to be stuck with such a kid in her class. He was a challenge both academically and socially. Academically, he was failing almost every class. It wasn't that he lacked the ability to do well; it was that he chose not to try. Socially, he was rude, mean, loud, rebellious, sneaky, and just about every other negative adjective one could conjure up. His ritual was to beat up at least one poor little soul a week. He was also known for torturing bugs when he had the chance, then making sure his classmates were shown the aftermath of the dead specimen. His classmates lived in fear of him.

He was the class—more specifically, the school—bully. After he had taken his aggression out on whoever the unfortunate victim would be for that particular day, he would be led down the frequent trek to the principal's office—while the unfortunate battered victim would be escorted to the first-aid room to patch up the injuries.

The door to her classroom abruptly swung open and a woman stood there. There wasn't even a question as to if the woman standing in front of her was Billy's mother. She was a spitting image of him in a female version. Rachel wondered if his mother had been a hellion when she was young.

Tall and gangly, she wore a bright red miniskirt that cut several inches above the knee and a tight white shirt littered with rhinestones under a faux fur coat. She topped it all off with red spiked heels. How she maneuvered herself around wearing them in the snow and ice was beyond Rachel. Her fingers sported long red nails with cheap gaudy rings, hideously decorating all ten. Her medium-length blonde frazzled hair had obviously befriended the peroxide bottle a few too many times.

"Hello, I'm Vivian—Billy's mother," she said swaggering in. She smacked her gum loudly and shamelessly between her blinding garish red lipstick. She did not extend her hand out, just expressed a slow provocative slide into the chair opposite Rachel. She sized Rachel up with her large green eyes that were decorated with a green shadow that glittered with every blink of her eyes. It reminded Rachel of the color she used to wear in junior high school. Vivian slid off her coat then crossed her arms over her ample chest, which Rachel determined was not heaven sent. As she crossed one leg over the other, Rachel noticed a tattoo on one ankle—a rose with its stem piercing through a heart.

Before she could address Vivian, a nice looking man who looked nothing like Billy, entered. He was wearing a slate gray business suit with a black-and-green striped tie over a white shirt. He had salt-and-pepper hair that was neatly parted on the side. His angular features made him quite handsome.

"Hello," he said. "I'm Grant Cooper." He extended his arm to shake Rachel's hand. Rachel politely held out her hand. He sat down cautiously in the chair next to Vivian, staring at her as if he feared for his life. Vivian didn't even acknowledge his presence. Instead, she stood up and dragged her chair away from him, creating an uncomfortable distance between the two. Rachel would have to address them separately.

"It is very nice to meet you, Mr. Cooper," Rachel said, then turned her head to Vivian. "Mrs. Cooper."

Vivian smacked her gum louder, fluttering her lashes. "Oh, honey, please do not insult me. My name is now Ms. Smith, soon to be *Mrs. Parker*," she said with a strong emphasis on her future name. She then glanced at Mr. Cooper with eyes as evil as Satan. Mr. Cooper continued to look straight ahead at Rachel without so much as a flinch.

"Well, to get down to business, how is my Billy doing . . . in spite of a *hostile* divorce I might add?" Vivian asked, waving her hand airily. The soon-to-be Mrs. Parker then crossed her arms and drummed her fingers on opposite arms. *Oh my god, who is this person?* Rachel asked herself.

"Sure, Ms. Smith," Rachel responded quickly,

"You can call me Vivian," she snapped.

"Oh yes, uh, excuse me, Vivian."

"Mr. Cooper," Rachel said, turning her head toward him with a pleasant smile. "I need to be right up front with both of you." She prepared herself for the backlash she knew would come—at least from Vivian. "Billy is failing in most of his subjects right now," Rachel said as respectfully as she could muster, maintaining her composure. She would have rather asked them what they had done, or not done, to create such a brat.

Mr. Cooper looked at Rachel with genuine concern. "In what subjects is he failing?" he asked. Vivian, sighed loudly and rolled her eyes, making it obvious she was annoyed by his question.

Rachel turned back to Mr. Cooper. "Uh—let's see," Rachel said, flipping through Billy's file. "Math, Spelling, Science, and Language Arts. Have you been receiving the progress reports or the e-mails I've sent you over the past few weeks?"

Vivian piped in before Mr. Cooper even had a chance to open his mouth. "Ms. Carter, you must understand that Billy's father doesn't spend any time reviewing anything that has to do with Billy's schooling. He doesn't care because he spends all his time boozing it up with his buddies and chasing twenty-year-old bimbos around town."

"Vivian! That is enough! You know that is not true," he responded tirelessly, as if he had explained this to her a hundred times. "I am not out boozing around." He then looked at Rachel, feeling compelled to explain. "I work in sales, and I have a lot of client dinners, that's all."

He did look sincere, and Rachel believed him. Mr. Cooper didn't seem like the kind of man who would be a player—although Rachel would have understood if he had been considering the obvious. What was this seemingly intelligent man thinking when he slipped a wedding ring on the finger of such an obviously psychotic bitch?

Vivian broke out laughing, "C'mon, Grant, be honest—that is the same excuse you have used for years, and you know as well as I do, it's a blatant lie!"

Mr. Cooper finally jerked his head toward Vivian, struggling to reel in his fractured temper. "Vivian, stop it! This is not the time or place for us to be discussing our . . ."

Vivian rudely cut in, "*You* are the one . . ."

Rachel had had enough. "Please—Vivian, Mr. Cooper, with all due respect, can we just focus on Billy's schoolwork?"

"Exactly!" Mr. Cooper agreed, turning toward Vivian.

"Whatever," she said, rolling her eyes once again. What sweet revenge it would be for Mr. Cooper if Vivian's eyes remained stuck like that for eternity. Rachel was appalled at her behavior. No wonder Billy had turned out so screwed up.

"OK," Rachel said, relieved. "I am going to give you both some guidelines here and exercises that you can work with Billy on so he can get to where he needs to be." She handed each parent some stapled forms. Vivian snatched hers and glanced at it like it was just one more irritating obstacle to deal with in her life.

"Thank you, Ms. Carter, this should help. I appreciate it," Mr. Cooper said.

Rachel patiently went over Billy's grades with them and explained the guidelines and exercises. Rachel then transitioned into what she knew would be even more of a difficult discussion.

"OK—now let's talk a bit about Billy's behavior," she said, clearing her throat. "He does tend to be disruptive in class, and the children are afraid of him because he is very abusive—both physically and verbally."

They both stared at her in disbelief. "Well," Vivian said, fuming. "I am sure that if he is being abusive, it's in response to being provoked by other kids—he is not the kind of person to hurt people." Rachel just gave her a brief smile, not wanting to get into an argument with a woman she knew would rip her apart.

Mr. Cooper, on the other hand, took a much more mature approach. "I will certainly talk to him about this, Ms. Carter. In fact, do you have the parents' phone numbers to the kids he has caused problems with? I will make sure that Billy calls them and apologizes for his actions."

"Just like you, Grant," Vivian exploded. "Throw Billy under the bus before you have the facts. Blame him for a situation you know nothing about."

The tension had reached its peak. Rachel focused on wrapping up the meeting as soon as possible. "I can send you an e-mail with that information if you would like, Mr. Cooper," Rachel said, grabbing a piece of paper and pen.

"Great," Mr. Cooper said as he dug his wallet out of his back pocket and pulled out a business card. "Here's my card. My e-mail address is at the bottom."

"OK—well I think that is it for now," Rachel said, clasping her hands together on top of her desk, thankful that the nightmare was ending. Vivian huffed like a child who had just had her favorite toy ripped away. She stood up, grabbed her coat, swirled around on her heels, and stormed out without looking back.

Mr. Cooper stood up and extended his hand. "Thank you so much for your help." Rachel smiled. He turned around, but then turned back to her. "I am very sorry for all the drama," he said apologetically, swirling his pointer finger next to his ear.

"It's OK," Rachel responded sympathetically. "I think I understand."

Shaking his head, he kindly responded, "With all due respect, Ms. Carter, I don't think you do."

Rachel hoped he had a restraining order against the woman. Who knows what was in the future for the poor man—for Billy. The image of Vivian hurling one of her red spiked heels at Mr. Cooper, impaling him straight through the forehead, flashed through her mind. There was no hope for Billy Cooper.

Chapter 17

"Hi, Monica, number three is about to happen. I had a dream last night," Rachel said.

"Oh god. We need to let Parchelli know right away," she said urgently. "Do you have any idea who the woman is?"

"No I don't, but I'm sure of one thing . . . she's in danger."

"Yes, there's no doubt about that," Monica concurred.

"I don't really know how, but we need to find out who she is," Rachel warned.

"Did you get a good look at her?" Monica asked, tapping her pencil rapidly on her desk.

"Yes. The lighting was pretty good. She has some Asian in her. She looked like she may be half Asian and half Caucasian."

"Do you think you could describe her to Brett and get a good sketch?"

"Yes," Rachel said. "Her description is pretty fresh in my mind though, so I need to meet with him soon."

"Definitely. Give Parchelli a call right now and get that set up," Monica instructed.

"OK, I'll call him."

"I'll give him a call as well to follow up. I think we have both learned that your dreams are not to be taken lightly, so the sooner you call him, the better. Let's see if we can find this bastard before this next one dies," Monica cautioned.

"I'll let Ted know I can meet with him right after school today," Rachel said. "I know it's important, but I can't keep missing work."

Rachel sat across from Parchelli, who held a grave expression. "We need to get you in front of Brett right away since this woman's face is fresh in your mind," he insisted.

"I agree. I think I can give him a pretty good description of her."

"Good. We need that more than anything right now," he said. Rachel noticed beads of sweat starting to accumulate on his forehead.

Rachel's heart was throttling in her chest as Parchelli led her down the hall to Brett's office.

Once again, she found herself gazing into Brett's beautiful gray eyes. God, he was beautiful. He looked even more handsome today than the first time she saw him. He had on a forest green sweater and black pants. Rachel had dressed up special for her meeting with Brett, wearing black pants snug enough to show off her toned figure and a pink sweater that followed her curves nicely.

"Hello again," Brett reached out his hand and gave her that million-dollar smile. She appreciated that he shook her hand just like he would a man and not like a fragile piece of china like some men do.

"Hi, Brett," was all she could squeak out of her vocal chords. Her heart was fluttering like the wings of a hummingbird.

"Ted says we have a woman to sketch this time. A potential victim?"

"Yes. I think I can give you a really good idea of what she looks like," Rachel said.

"Please sit down. Would you like some coffee?"

"You know, that sounds really good."

"I'll be back in a flash," he said, standing up from his desk. As he walked away, she turned to check him out. *Yummy.*

A few minutes later, he returned with two steaming mugs and handed one to Rachel, then he walked over and sat down at his desk. She wished she were sitting across from him at a nice restaurant rather than at the police station.

"So another dream about this psycho, huh?"

"Yes. It's the same killer. He butchers her just like he did Lisa and Danielle—same MO," Rachel explained.

"Wow," Brett shook his head. "This guy's a real gem, isn't he?"

"Yeah, no kidding."

"I can't imagine having these types of nightmares. I wouldn't even want to go to sleep at night."

"Yeah, especially because I have them every night."

"Every night? I didn't know that."

"When I'm not dreaming about somebody else getting killed by this freak, it's me who's getting murdered by him."

"You poor thing," Brett said, shaking his head. "Hopefully, we'll get him before he does anything else."

"That's what I'm hoping for. I don't want to die at such a young age."

"Of course not, you seem to have a lot going for you."

Rachel just smiled.

"The good thing here is that I can sketch women just as accurately as I can men. So . . . let's get started," Brett said, grabbing his pad and pencils. "OK, I'm ready whenever you are. Again, let's start with the shape of her face."

Rachel didn't need to be prompted this time on what he meant. "Her face was kind of oval shaped."

"OK, Ted was saying that she's Asian, or at least partially," Brett said while he started to sketch the shape of her face. Tell me about her facial features, starting with the eyes."

"Well, they were almond shaped."

"Were they dark colored?" he asked.

"Yes, they were dark brown."

He took a moment to sketch her eyes and noted on the side of the pad the eye color.

He passed the sketch to Rachel and she viewed the eyes. "They're a little more almond shaped."

He erased and drew the eyes again. After a few more tweaks, Brett stopped sketching and lifted the pad for Rachel to study more clearly.

"Yes, yes that's it," Rachel said. "Perfect."

Brett smiled without saying anything. "Let's move on to the next. What about her nose?"

"She had a straight nose, narrow at the bottom."

He continued to sketch the face. By the time he was done sketching the entire face, Rachel again was very impressed. "That's good, that looks very much like her."

"OK then," Brett said. "I'll run this over to Parchelli and see where he wants to go from here."

"Great," Rachel responded.

"Hey, have you had dinner yet?"

Rachel couldn't believe what she was hearing. *Did he just ask me out?*

"No, I haven't eaten," she responded a little too eagerly.

"Would you like to join me for dinner?"

"Sure, I . . . I would love that!" she said bubbling over with excitement.

Brett reached for the small of Rachel's back as he guided her into Anthony's Home Port restaurant. The lighting was dim; and the smell of steak and seafood, as well as Brett's cologne, made her mouth water.

The hostess led them to a table for two edged up against a window, giving them an incredible view of Puget Sound. The orange glow of the sun setting over the crisp horizon just added to the romantic atmosphere. Sitting on the table that was elegantly draped in white linen was a candle, gently flickering inside an etched glass vase.

In the middle of the dining area was a large fireplace that crackled and popped cedar wood. "This is sure cozy," Brett said, peering into the roaring flames.

"Especially on a day like this," Rachel added. "I just can't believe how cold it's been."

"Yeah, no kidding," Brett responded, rubbing his hands together.

Then a tall, slim waitress, who had dark brown hair that was pulled back with a gold clip, approached the table and handed them two hardbound menus.

"Hello, I'm Michelle, and I'll be your waitress this evening. You guys certainly have the best seat in the house tonight," she said with a huge smile, dimples appearing on her face. Another facial feature Rachel had always wished for.

"Yes, we feel special," Brett said, winking at Rachel.

A warm sensation travelled through Rachel that had nothing to do with the crackling fire.

"Our special entrée tonight is Shrimp Scampi, and our soup of the day is French Onion," the waitress said. "So I'll give you guys a few minutes to decide on dinner, but in the meantime, what can I bring you to drink?"

"I'll have a glass of Riesling," Rachel said, looking up at the waitress who was ogling Brett, obviously also enamored with him.

"That sounds good to me too, in fact, let's just make it a bottle," Brett said, looking at Rachel, "Is that OK with you?"

"Oh, absolutely," she quickly agreed. *The more alcohol, the more at ease I'll feel,* she thought to herself.

As the waitress sauntered off Rachel said, "I think the waitress is smitten with you."

"Now why would you say that?"

"Didn't you see the way she looked at you?"

"I didn't notice. I guess I was too busy looking at you," Brett said, raising his eyebrows.

"Were you now?" Rachel responded cocking an eyebrow.

Brett just smiled. "So tell me about yourself, Rachel," Brett asked her, his gray eyes twinkling and alluring in the dim light.

"Well . . . let's see . . . I'm a sixth-grade teacher," she said, placing the linen napkin on her lap. "I live in Kirkland. I've lived in the northwest for about eighteen years now, and I used to have an accent like you."

"Really? And why is that?" he said, emphasizing "*why*" in full southern as he unrolled his silverware and placed the napkin on his lap.

"Because I used to live in *Huntsv'll* and *y'all* talk like that down there," Rachel responded in her best southern drawl. "In fact, the longer I spend time with you, the more I'll be sounding just like you. Not to mention my accent thickens in direct accordance with how much alcohol I drink."

As if on cue, the waitress came back with the wine. After she left, Brett lifted his glass. "A toast from one southerner to another . . . may the accent thicken," he said, smiling.

"Are you trying to get me tipsy, Mr. Ryder?"

"Maybe," he said with a sly crooked grin, raising his glass to his lips, not taking his eyes off of her.

Chapter 18

The next morning, Rachel's head ached. She had a wonderful time with Brett last night at dinner and had invited him back to her house for a nightcap. She definitely got tipsy, and her southern accent was in full swing by the time she went to bed. She remembered most of the night. In spite of being a bit tipsy, she was glad she didn't say anything stupid. At least she didn't think she had, so that was good. They did kiss though, and it was fabulous. Electric sparks were flying every which way every time their lips touched.

She was downing two aspirins with a large glass of water when the phone rang. "Rachel, Ted Parchelli here," Ted spoke with a dry authoritative voice.

"Oh, hi, Ted. Did you look at the sketch?"

"Yes. That's what I want to talk to you about. It's quite interesting what we have here. Can you swing by the station today sometime?"

"Sure, I can stop by on my way home from work this afternoon."

Rachel walked into the station and Perma-Hair was sitting at the front desk, scowling. "Ted's on the phone right now, so I'll let him know you're here as soon as he hangs up," she snapped.

Rachel waited for Ted for about fifteen minutes. Finally, he came out to greet her. Rachel thought he looked tired. She had no idea how old he was, but she guessed he probably looked much older than he actually was. She surmised that doing a job like his would make you grow old fast. She couldn't imagine dealing with death and crime every day. Reflecting back on her teaching career, though she loved it, could sometimes make her feel like she had just ran a marathon by the end of the day, and she was only dealing with sixth graders.

She wasn't sure what he meant by "interesting" and was anxious to find out. Ted didn't smile at her, but he wasn't wearing the grumpy face he usually had toward her either. Maybe she was making progress with him. It was hard to tell.

"Hey, thanks for coming in. Please follow me," he said, waving his hand toward the hall as he turned around and walked. She followed him to his office and found herself focusing on his bald head bobbing up and down again.

"Have a seat," he told her, motioning toward the chair. Once again, she sat in the chair that was in desperate need of replacement. His office was still very much disorganized—more work in his "in" basket than in his "out" basket. The poor guy was a prime candidate for a heart attack.

He swiveled to grab a file behind his desk. Placing the manila folder in front of him, he looked straight at her. He was becoming more and more intimidating to Rachel the longer he stared at her, and she was starting to feel very uncomfortable. *What was going on now?* Rachel wondered. The stare he was giving her was eerie. Finally, he spoke. "You have quite the talent, Ms. Carter," he said, speaking over his large black-rimmed glasses. He looked down at the folder and opened it. He took out a piece of paper and laid it on his desk, facing Rachel. The woman in the photo staring back at her chilled her to the bone, and she felt a shutter slink down her spine.

The black-and-white photo on the missing person's flier was the woman in Rachel's dream. "Oh my god," Rachel said.

"Yes, Penny Norman," Ted said, his mouth tightening with determination. "This woman has been missing for a few weeks now."

"Wow," was the only thing Rachel could think to say.

"Yes. *Wow*, that's what I said as well."

Ted kept his eyes on Rachel. "Like I said, quite the talent."

"If she's been missing for that long, she's probably already dead. I must've dreamed about her after it happened," Rachel said, confused.

"She's been missing for a long time, but that doesn't necessarily mean she's been dead for a long time."

Oddly, Rachel felt blood rush to her face. "I don't know what to say," she responded.

"It looks like you are her voice, hopefully her savior. If we don't catch him in time, at least you'll be the passageway to her justice."

He reached for the flier and put it back in the file. "I think we know what's going to happen to her if it hasn't already."

"Yes, I think you're right. I hope she's still alive, but unfortunately if she's not, she met with just as grisly of an end as Lisa and Danielle."

"And who's to say these three women are the only ones he's killed in this area," Ted added. "We're going to find this bastard. I have a feeling he's right around the corner."

"I'm glad I could help you." A distressed smile spread across her face. "But each dream I have makes me more nervous. It just makes it that much closer to me being his next victim."

"I understand, Rachel," he said, waving the file around, "But rest assured that we are doing everything we can to find him. We've been able to get some good DNA samples from the crime scenes."

"What have you gotten so far?"

"I can't go into all the details of that, but one thing we found was a footprint in the snow. We know his shoe size."

"I imagine it's huge," Rachel said.

"Quite."

"He's a big man. No match for these poor women."

"True, but when we apprehend him, he will meet his match. He'll have to deal with me."

Chapter 19

Kristin Townsend lived a hard life. Both her mother and her father ended up alcoholics, who took their frustrations out on her as well as each other. They hadn't always been alcoholics, but just the hard knocks and a few unexpected curveballs that life had thrown their way had turned them both toward the bottle for comfort.

As a result, Kristin grew up in the midst of constant screaming, slamming objects against walls, and her dad beating the shit out of her mom. He was usually in a drunken state when he did it. A mean drunk.

It wouldn't be out of his character to beat Kristin in his drunken state over stupid things. One time, he came storming into her room, screaming about how she had left her school backpack on the kitchen counter. Other times, he beat her just because. Her mother, usually drunk herself, never defended her.

One thing she knew for sure—she would never follow in the footsteps of her parents. Alcohol was out of the question. She saw firsthand the damage it caused.

When things became too unbearable and she felt like she was old enough, Kristin left. She was only sixteen, but if she could survive the hell she had lived in, she would be able to survive anything on the streets. Not graduating from high school was no concern of hers—at least not then.

Without an education, she learned to survive by walking the streets and becoming a prostitute. It was a scummy and a lowlife way of living, but it was better than living in fear of a father who would beat her repeatedly for no reason at all. She had a pimp that cared more for her safety than her father ever had.

Having been a prostitute for quite some time, she wanted to clean up her life to some extent. Not that exotic dancing was the most reputable way to make a living, but at least it was better than prostitution. She hit the streets to look for an opportunity.

Under her short black leather coat, she wore a tight, low-cut red shirt and a denim miniskirt. The black platinum-leather spiked heels she topped it all off with were not conducive considering the weather, but considering her so-called career, it was part of the gig. She let her blonde hair flow free and had applied heavy makeup on her face. She hated men for being such perverts.

The first exotic club she saw—*Honeysuckles*—was as good as any place to start. She couldn't see anything at first when she walked inside because the place was so dark, and her eyes were still adjusting from the sunlight outside. She did hear, however, a bunch of whistling directed her way. After her eyes had adjusted, she saw a man standing mere feet from her. He looked like he had just crawled out of a dumpster. He was shorter than she was, had big bloodshot bug eyes, and all the hair that should've been on his head had decided to nest on his shoulders and neck. He was dressed in a grungy wife-beater tank top and jeans that looked like they hadn't been washed in weeks.

"Well hello, darlin'. I'm Lou, the manager," he smiled, baring crooked yellow teeth. Between his teeth and his breath, she figured he was a chain smoker, or close to it.

She noticed him undressing her with his eyes from top to bottom, making no effort to hide his lust. It didn't offend her—she was used to it. She was stunningly beautiful with long blonde hair, striking eyes, and a body that would arouse any straight man.

He liked what he saw. He had been in the business long enough to know which girls brought in the most money, and Kristin was definitely in that category.

"Looking for a job, sweetie?" Lou asked, swaggering even closer.

"Uh, well, I'm just checking a few places out and . . . ," she said, stepping back away from him.

"Like I said, you're looking for a job," Lou growled lustily. "Baby, anyone who looks like you is meant for this type of job. Wanna make lots of money?"

"How much money?" Kristin asked a bit shamefully.

"I'd say for someone with your *assets*," emphasizing the word *ass*, "How does about ten grand a month sound?"

Kristin was shocked and covered her mouth with one hand. "What?"

"You heard me, baby, about ten grand a month. That's including tips that'll go right in your pocket—or shall I say in your . . ." He shamelessly looked down at her cleavage and then up to her eyes again.

The money was about five times what she had figured. "Well . . . I mean . . . how do you know how much I'll make in tips?" she asked him, shifting her weight and taking another step back.

"Baby, I have been in this business for over twenty years and have managed this place for ten of them," he bragged. "I've had all types of girls over the years, and their ain't many as pretty as you. Just try it. Say . . . give it a month and see for yourself."

"Well . . ."

"What? Ten grand a month ain't enough for ya?" he scoffed. "I doubt any other place would be so generous."

"When would I be able to start if I were to take the position?"

"Anytime you would like to. But I have one more question before that can happen," he said as a wicked smile spread across his face. "You see that ten grand I was talking about—there is something that you need to be OK with."

"What's that?" she asked, with all sorts of things racing through her mind.

He looked at her provocatively as he pulled out a cigarette from the pack he was carrying and lit it. "You gotta dance nude," he said, taking a deep drag.

"Uhm . . . ," she hesitated.

"Ten grand, baby—that's a real nice chunk of change, don't ya think? It could buy you lots of nice things," he said alluringly.

"OK," she finally said. "But there's one thing you need to know about me beforehand also." He raised his eyebrows instead of asking a question. "I've never danced nude before, I—"

"No problem, sugar," he cut her off. "I have lotsa girls here that can teach ya. Believe me honey pie, the boys in here," he said, thumbing back at the men still staring at her. "They ain't gonna be looking at your dancing, if ya know what I mean. Come on in tomorrow afternoon, say around two, and I can have Candy work with ya on the pole."

She didn't have a choice unless she kept searching, and the money was something she couldn't pass up. "Well, all right. I guess I can give it a try," she said.

"Good choice," he growled, grinding out his cigarette in an ashtray sitting on the nearest table. Seconds after she turned to leave, Lou gave the boys a thumbs-up and they all hooted and hollered like they had just won the lottery. "I better get used to it," she quietly muttered to herself. "I better get real used to it."

Chapter 20

Rachel downed two aspirins with her lukewarm coffee. It was a Monday, and as on every Monday, she knew school would be a little tougher today than most days. The kids filed in slowly and quietly. Most of them had frowns on their faces. They looked like Rachel felt. No one wanted to be there—not one. They looked like a herd of multicolored cotton balls scrambling through the door with their heavy winter coats, scarves, and gloves. There was still a lot of snow on the ground, and with the freezing temperatures remaining, it wasn't going away anytime soon.

Once the kids got settled in, Rachel put a fake smile on her face, hoping the kids could muster up the same so they could all get through the grueling day. It didn't happen.

Recess finally came and the kids scurried out the door as fast as possible. Rachel felt the chill. She shivered. She didn't know if it was because of the temperature outside or the way Billy was staring her down. He sat in his seat with no intention of moving an inch. Rachel was uncomfortably perplexed. Billy usually bullied himself to the door first whenever it was time for recess.

After a long silence, Rachel spoke. "Is there something wrong, Billy?"

He cocked his head, and with an evil smirk, said, "I don't know, Ms. Carter. Is there?"

"What's going on? Is there a problem you want to talk to me about?"

"I don't have a problem, but I think you do."

"What . . . what are you talking about?" Rachel asked, confused.

"You know that bad guy who is killing all those girls—The . . . *Heart . . . break . . . Killer*," he said, pausing between each word.

"Yes, what about him?" Rachel asked as her head started to spin.

"He did terrible things to those poor girls. I bet he's going to kill you too," he said, sneering.

"Billy, why would you say something like that?"

"Just be careful. You never know what can happen," Billy warned, getting up from his chair. He walked to the coat rack and put on his coat. Turning back toward her, he gestured slitting his throat again.

A shudder rushed through Rachel's body. This was insane, she thought. *What the hell was that all about? Does he know something I don't?*

Rachel hoped she had made the right decision to ask Brett over for dinner. Although she wasn't a gourmet cook, she did know how to throw together spaghetti, French bread, and a salad.

The doorbell rang and she took one last glance at herself in the bathroom mirror before she sprinted for the door. She had taken more time getting ready than she had with other dates because, well, there was just something special about Brett.

She was wearing black leggings, black leather boots, and a long—sleeved brown sweater cinched at the waist with a black belt. "Hi," she said, glowing, as she invited Brett in.

"You look absolutely stunning," Brett complimented her with an infectious smile.

"Thanks," she said gently, putting her hand on his arm. "So do you."

He wore a well-worn pair of jeans that had a sexy way of fitting him and a white long-sleeved shirt that hung loosely over them. His cologne, once again, made her knees weak.

"Would you like a drink?" Rachel asked as she led him into the kitchen.

"Sure, what do you have?"

"I've got both red and white wine, vodka, beer."

"A glass of white wine would be wonderful," he said.

"Chardonnay or Riesling?"

"Riesling, of course."

"Just like the other night. Sounds good to me," she said.

He sat down at the kitchen table as she pulled the bottle from the fridge and uncorked it.

"Whatever you are making smells delicious."

"Nothing special. Spaghetti."

Handing him the glass, their hands lightly touched and Rachel felt a buzz shoot through her from head to toe.

"I absolutely love spaghetti."

"Good. We're having French bread and salad with it."

"Sounds delicious."

She walked back over to the stove, picked up the wooden spoon, and started to stir the sauce that was simmering on the burner.

"When did you first know you were psychic?" he asked.

She opened the cupboard and pulled out a bowl to pour the sauce into.

"Well, do you remember the plane that crashed last Christmas Eve?"

"Yeah, the one that went down over the ocean?"

"Yes. I dreamt about that a few weeks before it happened," she said nervously.

"Really?"

"Yes, I dreamt about every gory detail," Rachel said, pouring the sauce from the stove to the bowl. She placed the bowl on the table. Then she walked over and grabbed the spaghetti, the salad, and the French bread.

"That must've been awful," Brett said as she sat down.

"It was, but I didn't realize I was psychic at the time. I just thought it was some weird fluke or something."

"Yeah, but you still must've been freaked out."

"I was. But then I didn't have any other predictions, so I kind of just let it to," she said, taking a sip of her wine, relishing the fruity alcohol tantalizing her taste buds.

"I've always thought it would be kind of cool to be psychic."

Rachel shook her head, passing Brett the salad. "It's not, believe me. The visions I have are not worth it."

"So can you read minds too?" he asked warily.

"Are you wondering if I can read your mind right now?" she asked playfully.

"Well . . . I was just wondering," Brett said, pouring some dressing over his salad.

"Yes, as a matter of fact, I do know what you are thinking right now," Rachel teased.

"No, really, can you read minds?" he asked, worry started to cloud his eyes.

"No, I can't read minds—you can relax," she smiled, handing him the bowl of spaghetti.

"That's good!"

"Why is that?" Rachel asked, sprinkling some Parmesan over her spaghetti.

"Hmm," Brett responded, raising an eyebrow.

"Hmm, what?" Rachel pried.

"I was just thinking how beautiful you are," he said, raising his wine glass toward her to toast. *Clink.*

Rachel was awestruck. "Well, you're not so bad yourself."

"I guess we have a mutual admiration club then," Brett said, laughing.

"I guess so. Here's to the mutual admiration club," Rachel said, raising her glass to him for another toast.

"Are you still having the dreams about yourself?" Brett asked, changing the subject, his face becoming more serious.

Rachel's face clouded over. "Yes. They're the worst ones."

"Well, don't worry. We're going to catch this guy way before anything happens to you. I can assure you of that."

"I hope so," she shrugged. "There's not much I can do about that."

"Yes you can," Brett said, reaching for a slice of French bread. "You can keep letting us know your predictions." Brett then reached over to Rachel and put his hand on top of hers. She felt the electricity jolt through her body. "I know I'm going to do everything possible myself to help the police catch him."

"I just find myself always looking over my shoulder, ya know?" Rachel said, filling his glass with more wine.

"Well, nothing is going to happen to you when I'm around, I guarantee you of that," he smiled warmly.

Dracula sauntered up to Brett's chair and began rubbing himself around his feet.

"You have an admirer," Rachel said.

"Yes. I guess we're going to have to add one more to our admiration club."

"You know, Brett, I really like you," Rachel said, stretching her neck out on the notorious limb.

"You know, Rachel, I really like you too."

"That's a good thing then."

"That's a good thing," Brett agreed, raising his glass for yet another toast.

"I just feel so comfortable around you, it's weird."

"I feel the same way. It's like we've known each other all our lives," he said, rolling his spaghetti around his fork. "By the way, I love this spaghetti."

"Good. I was worried. I'm not that great of a cook."

"Well, you're certainly good at cooking spaghetti," he said, his gray eyes smoldering.

"Now, on to you . . . ," Rachel said. "Have you always known you wanted to be a sketch artist?"

"No. I've just always loved to draw."

"You are very good at it," Rachel complimented.

"Thanks. It's what I love to do," Brett winked.

"I can't even draw a stick man." Rachel laughed, twirling some spaghetti on her own fork.

"I guess we all have our talents. I can't imagine being a schoolteacher—now *that* takes talent."

"Not really talent, just patience."

"Do you ever lose your patience?"

"Sure I do, I just have to be careful not to show it," Rachel smiled.

"Yes, nowadays, Child Protective Service comes running if you look at a kid wrong."

"True. We have to be careful when we discipline them. Sometimes I feel like throttling them," Rachel said, rolling her eyes.

"I bet. So do you have any particular students that drive you crazy?"

"Yes, I have one little psycho."

"Do tell . . ."

"His name is Billy, and he's the school bully. He even bullies me," Rachel said, shaking her head.

Brett put his fork down. "How's that?"

"It's interesting, but it's almost like he's psychic too," Rachel said, her eyebrows knitted together.

"Really? What does he do to make you think that?"

"The other day, he actually gestured slitting his throat and told me that I should beware of the Heartbreak Killer," Rachel said, shuddering.

"That's creepy."

"Yeah, no kidding."

"It's probably just a coincidence," Brett comforted. "Everyone has heard about the Heartbreak Killer and everyone seems to be talking about him. He probably heard it on the news or heard his parents talking about it."

"I know," Rachel said. "It just hits a little too close to home I guess."

Brett reached for Rachel's hand again. "We're going to get this whacko before he kills again."

After dinner, Brett and Rachel sat down on the couch to watch a movie on cable. He put his arm around her and immediately pulled her close to him. It was so natural to be around Brett. There was none of that awkward-first-date feel. It really was like they had been together for years.

Chapter 21

Rachel was having a hard time falling asleep. She feared having another dream. It was midnight, and she knew she needed to get up early the next morning, so she made a cup of her mother's famous tea. She sipped it slowly, desperately hoping it was as miraculous as her mother had claimed. Once she felt sleepy enough, she put the book down that she was reading and switched off the light. But only because she had to . . .

Rachel peered down from her perch and saw Randall sitting at Duke's Diner. His thoughts tore through her mind.

He waited patiently for Natalie to come back as he sat in the booth he always sat in. He had been considering her as his next victim for a while now. His mother had been pushing him toward her. She was pretty, lean, long legged. Why she was working as a waitress at Duke's and not sauntering down a runway as a model was a mystery to him, he thought as he drummed his fingers on the side of his coffee cup.

Natalie had waited on him several times before and was always so pleasant. Why did his mother have to choose someone like Natalie? It made it much more difficult to murder someone he knew, especially someone who was nice to him.

"More coffee?" she asked with her sweet little voice.

"Yes, please," Randall responded, eyeing her carefully. He watched her long fingers grasp the coffeepot tightly and pour the hot steaming liquid into his cup.

He looked up into her pretty face—beautiful big blue eyes and long brown hair that was pulled back into a tight knot at the back of her head. She was wearing her usual restaurant attire—a dirt brown-colored skirt, a beige top, and a black apron wrapped around her small waist. He found it ironic that such a dull, mundane uniform could look so good on someone.

She glanced at him with a wholesome genuine smile. No pretense. Not fake—like so many other women he had encountered.

He made sure not to get too close to her. He knew he would eventually have to kill her. His mother was relentless when she chose her victims.

"How have you been, Randall?" Natalie asked.

"So your name is Randall, huh? I've got you now, you bastard. I have your name!" Rachel said.

"I've been good, Natalie, and you?"

"Busy," she responded, rolling her eyes and shaking her head.

Tonight was the night. He would eat, leave, wait for her to get off work, and then follow her home.

201

"A poor, innocent waitress—and one who's been so nice to you all this time. How long are you going to keep killing?" Rachel asked, knowing he couldn't hear her.

After Randall had eaten, he stood up, left a generous tip, and left. He had parked his car in a lot adjacent to the restaurant. Sitting in his car, he watched. He waited.

Rachel viewed the old, beat-up white Chevy Malibu below.

After her shift, Randall watched as Natalie gracefully sauntered to her car. God, she was a beauty. What a shame he would have to kill her tonight.

Rachel suddenly floated down and was now sitting in the car beside Randall. "So you're going to follow her home and kill her?" Rachel watched him. He was visibly shaken, visibly tormented. He was clenching the steering wheel like it was the only thing that kept him from falling into oblivion.

Natalie pulled into her driveway and Randall slowly eased his car up against the curb a few houses down. Rachel watched him strap on the death pack. After Natalie had let herself into the house, Randall got out and walked behind the houses so he wouldn't be spotted from the street. Rachel floated beside him.

"Don't do this!" Rachel pleaded.

He slid up alongside the front of Natalie's house and checked the front door. Unlocked. Things were in his favor. He quietly opened the door and saw Natalie standing in the kitchen.

"Randall, it's not worth it!" Rachel said as she floated beside him, knowing her words were futile.

I am a kind man. I am a gentle man. His mantra rang in his mind—in Rachel's mind.

Natalie felt the hairs on the back of her neck start to prickle. She felt the presence of someone behind her, but when she turned around, there was no one there. She turned back around, grabbed a glass from the cupboard, and turned on the water. Perfect time for him to make his move, he thought. Rachel just stared at him in utter terror.

"Turn around, Natalie!" Rachel screamed.

It was too late. Randall pounced and put his arm around Natalie's neck. She immediately gasped and dropped the glass of water onto the kitchen floor where it shattered.

"I'm sorry, Natalie. You must die tonight," Randall whispered in her ear.

Natalie knew his voice. "Randall? What are you doing?" she said as she struggled against him.

"You are the one my mother wants me to kill," he explained.

"Leave her alone!" Rachel pleaded.

"What the hell . . ." Natalie screamed.

The one thing Randall didn't know was that Natalie had a black belt in karate. She jabbed him in the ribs with her elbow. Doing so, she broke from his hold and kneed him in the groin with all her strength, causing him to bend over, incapacitated. That left her just enough time to run out to the neighbor's house.

"Good girl! Run!" Rachel screamed, "Run!"

"Help, help!" Natalie yelled, beating on her neighbor's door. The porch light went on and eighty-five-year-old Betty Foster opened the door cautiously. Betty stood there in her light pink checkered pajamas and matching slippers, confused and horrified.

"Dear, what in the world . . ." Betty started to ask in her high—pitched quivering voice. Before she could get the question out, Natalie pushed herself against Betty, forcing her back into the house. Natalie quickly turned around and locked the door.

"Make sure all your doors are locked!" Someone just tried to kill me!" Natalie said frantically, closing the drapes.

"Oh dear, oh dear," Betty responded, scurrying to the back of the house.

"Good girl, you got away!" Rachel cried as she floated beside Natalie. "Now go to the police. Let's nail this bastard. Call the police!"

"Monica, I had another dream last night," Rachel said.

"Oh dear god!"

"Wait, there's good news. She got away!"

"She got away from him? She's alive?"

"Yes. She must know martial arts or something because the moves she made on him incapacitated him pretty quickly. She was able to run out of her house and into a neighbor's house safely."

"Did she call the police?"

"I'm pretty sure. I woke up before that happened, but I'm sure she would. We'll need to check with Parchelli. Her name is Natalie and she works at Duke's Diner. The murderer's name is Randall. He's one of her regular customers there," Rachel explained. "He drives a white Chevy Malibu."

"That's awesome! Did you get the plate number?" Monica asked.

"No, I didn't see the plate."

"That's OK. They'll find him anyway with the information this Natalie woman has on him. Call Ted now!"

"I will. Maybe catching this beast is right around the corner."

"I think we have a good chance," Monica said. "I'm sure Natalie wants the nut found as well."

"I hope they can find him soon. He knows where Natalie lives. I'm sure she's afraid he'll come after her to finish her off."

"Did you get details on her house?" Monica asked. "Just in case she didn't contact the police, were you able to see her address—did you see any address numbers on the outside of her house?"

"All I saw was mainly what the house looked like inside. She didn't lock the door behind her and he followed her in. She was in the kitchen when he grabbed her—but it could've been anyone's kitchen. It was pretty much generic. Nothing really stood out to me," Rachel said.

"Do you know what area or neighborhood she lives in?" Monica asked putting her hand around her neck feeling it start to throb.

"No. I have no idea. God, I hope she contacted the police. I really do. She'd be crazy not to," Rachel said.

"I'm sure she's contacted them, Rachel. When most people are attacked and lucky enough to get away, they usually go straight to the police," Monica explained. "She saw his face. She knows who he is. He's exposed now. She'll be able to identify and describe him to the police."

"I hope so."

"It's good she knows his face. You said he's a regular at Duke's?"

"Yes. They seemed to know each other pretty well."

Rachel got Parchelli's voice mail. "Ted, call me as soon as you can. I had a dream about another woman who was attacked by the Heartbreak Killer, but she was able to get away from him. Have you heard from her? Call me. I have a lot of details on this one." She hung up the phone, breathless.

Within five minutes, the telephone rang. Rachel picked it up on the first ring.

"She came in late last night. We're all over it," Ted said. "Her name is Natalie Watson. She met with Brett this morning. The sketch matches the one you gave us almost exactly. We can now release the sketch to the public."

"Oh, I am so relieved," Rachel exhaled loudly. "Did she tell you that she knows him? She waitresses for him at Duke's Diner."

"Yes, she told me everything."

"In the dream, I saw that he drives an older white model Chevy Malibu. That could be another tip in helping to locate him."

"Awesome, that should help," Ted responded. "We've already contacted the media with the sketch and the name. Hopefully someone will recognize him and call in."

Chapter 22

'I knew you would screw up eventually,' he heard his mother's voice chastising him. Her face, as always, dripping with acid.

"Mother," he pleaded. "I'm sorry, I'm so sorry."

'Sorry? You're sorry?. For what—sorry for murdering me or sorry for letting that wench get away?' her voice droned on.

Randall bowed his head. "Sorry for everything, Mother—I'm sorry for everything," he repeated quietly. Pain started shooting through his brain. He squeezed his temples with his fingers, hoping for some relief. Once again, he avoided his mother's glare. Why couldn't he make her happy? So many girls dead, and yet she was still not satisfied.

Randall rarely took a stand with her, but he had reached his breaking point. "Mother, what about all the other girls? The other ones that I've killed for you? I've murdered so many, Mother—and they've all been for you."

Her phantom voice consumed him. *'Those girls? That was nothing, Randall—nothing! You think those girls make up for what you did to me? How dare you even think such a thing.'*

He crumbled to her venom and was overwhelmed by guilt. "You're right. Even if I kill a hundred more girls, it still won't make up for you dying."

'Make up for me dying? You mean make up for you murdering me.'

"I tried, Mother, I really did."

'Well, you didn't try hard enough, Randall.'

"Stop! Please stop! I can't take it anymore," Randall's voice bellowed out. "I can't please you no matter what I do. I keep killing women and you still can't forgive me."

Her gaze was intolerable. *'You're right on that one, Randall, you are so right. You are so stupid, Randall. So stupid.'*

"Mother, *you* were the one who chose Natalie, not me! How was I supposed to know she could defend herself like that? She took me by complete surprise."

'Randall, you are a big man. How could you let such a small woman overtake you? You may be a big man, but you are a very weak man. You're weak. You're pathetic.'

Randall put his head in his hands and wept.

Chapter 23

Rachel needed to get away from all the madness. It was a perfect time to take some time off work to clear her head, and more importantly, to evade the freak while the police followed up on the new leads. She felt confident that they would be moving in on him soon. They had the sketch, the eyewitness, his name, the car.

"I have a few days off work. I think I'm going to head out for a little solitary time," Rachel told her mom over the phone.

"Dear, where are you planning on going, and why on earth would you want to go somewhere alone?" her mother asked.

"I think I might head over to Friday Harbor. I just need some solitary time."

Friday Harbor was part of the San Juan Islands that scattered throughout Puget Sound. They were known for their quaint bed and breakfasts, hiking, kayaking and just plain relaxation. Rachel had been to them several times. Every so often, she would take a weekend to get away to one of the islands just to do something other than sit home grading her sixth graders' papers. It was a perfect getaway. She relished those times when she boarded one of the ferries after a tiring week and let her worries wash away in the ferry's wake.

"Are you still having those dreams?" Anita asked.

"Yes, but I'm not going to let that scare me. I just need to get away." The last thing Rachel was going to do was fill her mother in on the details of what was going on. Her mom was already worried sick about her.

"Well, OK, honey. But if you need me, I can maybe make arrangements for Carl to watch the boys and . . ."

Rachel didn't dare let her finish her sentence. "No, no, Mom. I'm fine. I need to be alone. Please . . ."

"OK, OK," Anita finally submitted.

Rachel could finally sigh with relief. The police should be hot on Randall's trail by now, and it couldn't be that hard to find him considering Natalie, the eyewitness could identify him, and the police now knew his name as well as the type of car he drives. Yes, she finally felt safe. She figured that her jaunt over to the San Juan Islands would be a great place to calm her raw nerves as well as keep her safe during the apprehension of Randall.

She had been shaken to the bone as far as being on Randall's murder list. She actually dodged that fatal bullet. Thank God. She suddenly felt a hollow ache within her heart, knowing that so many girls hadn't been so lucky and had ended up dead. Being able to save both Lisa and Danielle from their grisly fate was something she wished she had been able to do. If they had just found him earlier. The police had put forth their best effort to find him, she couldn't place blame on them. They had very little to go on and not enough time to find him.

As far as Randall, Rachel hoped he would burn in hell. She realized that he was obviously mentally ill, which caused his brain to function in a twisted fashion, but she would never forgive him for the blood trail he left behind. Lisa, the aspiring news reporter, had worked so hard to get to where she was with her career and she had so many aspirations for her future. Randall had robbed her of that. Danielle, who was just beginning to live, had so much promise. She rose above the egocentric world of a teenager and instead thought of the welfare of others. Her bright, wide smile, the big brown doe eyes. Gone. Randall took everything from her. Then Penny Norman, the missing Asian woman, wherever she was, had probably had her life cut short as well.

Yes, she was looking forward to catching the ferry that weekend. She couldn't wait to stand on the top deck of the boat and watch the seagulls fly above her, letting the wind determine their course. They may squawk loudly as if in protest to the unruly, cold winter air, but they would soar above her and they were free. Free. Like them, she finally felt free. Free from the terror, free from the worry.

Chapter 24

The police posted the sketches of Randall everywhere, hoping that someone could lead them to him. Natalie was an acquaintance of his, but she had no idea where he lived.

By then the description of the killer had been broadcast by all the television stations. The fliers were being distributed everywhere—local convenient stores, shopping malls, gas stations.

Having seen his sketch on the news, Randall knew it was only a matter of time before he was apprehended. He thought of getting in his car and just driving, but in a way he wanted to be captured. He was tired. Tired of killing, tired of having to evolve into someone he was not just to keep his mother's wrath at bay. How could his mother hold it against him if he was captured? It's not like he tried to get caught. It's not like he turned himself in or just stopped killing. Maybe her voice would now quiet, knowing there was nothing more he could do. He could run, but he knew he couldn't hide for long.

Besides, it was his mother who wanted Natalie dead, not him. So the blame was on her. How was he supposed to know that Natalie could fight back and get away? His mother should've picked someone else.

Anonymous tips were coming into the police like crazy. Many people had seen Randall's face. But the best lead came from Randall's employer; two days after the sketch had been broadcast.

"Ted Parchelli here," Ted answered the phone sharply.

"Uh, I think I've got your killer. You know the guy you're calling the Heartbreak Killer," a man's voice quietly and calmly spoke into his ear.

"Go on," Ted encouraged.

"Yeah, my name is Brian Tysen. I own Tysen's Construction. I hired him as a framer about a month ago. God, had I known . . ."

Ted cut him off. "Don't worry about that. I need a last name and an address."

"His name is Randall Metzgar," Brian said. The man gave Ted Randall's address. *Who knows if he's still there,* Ted thought. *But at least, it's a start.*

"Do you know the make and model of the car he drives?"

"Yes, I believe it's a white Chevy. I think a Malibu. Old and beat up."

"Would you happen to have the license plate number?"

"Uh, let's see here," Brian said. Parchelli could hear him shuffling through papers. "No, I don't have the plate number, but I remember he drove a white Chevy."

"That's OK. Just knowing that helps us."

"Yeah, I was wondering what happened to him. He hasn't shown up here at work for about a week now. Was gonna fire his ass if he ever showed his face again."

Ted hung up and sprinted from his office. "Boys, we may have just found where our killer is. Let's move on this now!" Ted commanded to his squad. "We need to move quick. He could be on the run by now."

Within two hours of receiving the tip, the police had surrounded Randall's apartment. They noticed the white Chevy Malibu parked in the lot, which was a good sign Randall still lived there, and they lucked out because it looked like he was home. Armed and ready, two police officers pounded on Randall's door. Expecting the worse, they had their guns drawn and snipers were zeroed in.

Randall sat in his apartment with his mother's picture facedown on the desk when he heard the knock at the door. He was ashamed, but there was nothing he could do now. Back and forth, back and forth he rocked. "I am a gentle man, I am a kind man," he repeated.

To their surprise, Randall gently opened the door and surrendered himself immediately without incident. He was whisked down to the station for questioning. He held his mother's picture in his hands.

In interrogation, Randall didn't do anything to hide his identity. He confessed to the recent murders, and when presented with a missing persons' list, identified some of those whose bodies had not yet been located—some in other states. He told the police that he would fully cooperate with them and lead them to where he had left what he called the "Beauties."

It had ended—it was over. A sense of relief overtook Randall. "Please know that they didn't die alone. I at least owed them that," he had insisted to the police. "You see, I comforted all of them until their dying breath."

"How thoughtful of you," Ted snarled.

When the police searched his apartment, they found the death pack and saw the bloody clothes, just as Randall had told them they would.

Chapter 25

"C'mon, girl," Anna Draker gave her Palomino horse, Lilly, a light whip, prompting her into a canter for her early morning exercise across the five-acre plot of land.

Once they came to a clearing, Anna saw something in the distance, lying beside the man-made pond her husband, Dylan, had dug for her last year. "What the heck?" Anna said out loud, having no idea what it was. As Lilly got closer, Anna thought it was a dead animal; but to her horror, she realized it was a dead body. It was a girl, and there was blood—lots of blood. She saw the wooden heart and chills went through her body. The Heartbreak Killer had tread upon her land and left a lifeless body in his wake.

"Monica, we have a bad situation here," Ted said.

"Now what?" she asked, resigned.

"Have you talked to Rachel lately?" Ted asked.

"No, I haven't spoken with her. The last time I talked with her was last week, just a few days before you brought Randall into custody. She told me she was taking a little vacation, over to the San Juan Islands. Now that I think about it, it is a little strange she hasn't called. I'm sure she's heard about his arrest by now. I mean, it's all over the news. I can certainly give her a call for you. I'm sure she'll call me back."

"Don't count on her calling you back."

"Why do you say that?" Monica asked warily, feeling her throat constrict.

"I think we found her body this morning, same MO."

"What?" Monica's heart stopped. "That doesn't make any sense, Randall's been arrested!"

"He must've murdered her right before we apprehended him. Sounds like bad timing to me."

"Are you sure it's her?" Monica asked, panicked.

"She's a dead ringer if it isn't her. I saw her myself. We'll do a DNA check and all, but I have no doubt. Her eyes were open, and they were definitely her eyes. I've never seen anyone else with eyes so shockingly pale blue. Her parents are heading to the morgue right now to ID her."

Monica felt her blood pressure soar. "Dear god," she gasped. "How can that be? I spoke to her just a few days before you found him."

"Like I said, bad timing. We did everything we could, Monica. I am so sorry."

"Do you know exactly when he killed her?"

"The coroner can't tell us exactly when she died until he does an autopsy. The body is very well preserved due to the cold weather. She was practically frozen solid. That's another reason I knew it was her. There was very little decomposition."

"Are you sure that it was Randall who murdered her?"

"Yes. Like I said, same MO. There was a wooden heart at the scene."

"Did he admit to killing her?"

"He admitted to killing several women, many of whom were blonde, but he didn't specifically tell us it was Rachel," Ted responded.

"Where was she found?" Monica's voice cracked with emotion.

"A woman out in Black Diamond found her this morning while riding her horse on her land. I spoke to Brett. He's devastated. Left the office."

Monica felt her blood pressure rise. "It would have been nice if you would've apprehended him before he got to her!"

Ted took a deep breath to bridle his own growing temper. "We did the best we could. We followed up on all the leads, and I'm sorry it took a few days to apprehend him, but that's how the system works," Ted said defensively.

"Dear god, I . . ." Monica's voice caught midsentence. "I thought we got him in time."

"So did I." Ted sighed. "I'm sorry."

"Not as sorry as I am," Monica said tersely. "You weren't the one who assured her that she was safe."

After Monica hung up the phone, she dropped her head in her hands. She had been wrong all along. How would she ever forgive herself for giving Rachel false hope? She was so confident that Rachel was safe.

The stench of formaldehyde and death filled the morgue as Carl and Anita entered. Carl held Anita up as she walked feebly up to the gurney. The body was covered with a white sheet. *It couldn't be Rachel, it just couldn't be.* It was so surreal. She had just talked to Rachel a few days ago—right before she left for vacation.

The coroner pulled the sheet back to expose the face. Her daughter's face, still beautiful, stared back at her. Anita covered her mouth with her hand and stepped back—dizziness overtaking her and then . . . *black.*

The next thing she knew was a vague sight of the coroner and Carl gently slapping her face, trying to get her to come to. She slowly remembered where she was and the horror returned with a vengeance. This was not a dream. Her baby girl was dead. Her beautiful baby girl's face intact, but her throat was nearly cut clean through.

"How could've this happened to our baby, Carl?" Anita cried uncontrollably.

Carl held his sobbing wife tightly in his arms as his teary eyes stayed glued on the still flawless face of his daughter.

"I don't know, honey, I don't know," he responded despondently.

"And in such a horrible way," Anita's voice trembled.

"I know. But one thing is for sure," he said, slamming his hand down on the steel gurney that held his daughter. "I'll make sure they fry this bastard if it's the last thing I do. He's going to pay for taking our baby away from us. He's going to pay."

Chapter 26

"Hi, Mom," Rachel spoke into the phone. There was a catch in Anita's breath and then silence. "Mom, are you there?" Still nothing. Rachel heard the phone drop, and then footsteps running away from the phone. "Carl! Carl!" Rachel heard her mother scream.

"Mom? Mom?" Rachel yelled into the phone, hearing a distant unrecognizable frantic discussion on the other end of the line.

The next thing she knew, her dad was on the phone. "Hello? Who is this!" he said angrily.

"Dad, what's going on?" Rachel asked, confused.

There was a pause. "Is this some kind of joke?" Carl asked, furious.

"Dad, what the *hell* is going on?" Rachel responded just as angry.

"This isn't funny! Who is this?" Carl demanded.

"It's Rachel, Daddy. What's going . . . why are you acting like this?"

Click. The phone went dead. Rachel couldn't believe what just happened. She found herself just staring into the receiver. Quickly, she dialed again.

"Hello!" her dad answered. He was livid.

"Daddy . . ."

"Who *is* this?" Carl growled into the phone.

"Dad, it's me. Who do you think it is?" Rachel laughed nervously.

Recognizing her voice this time, he asked, "*Rachel?* Is it really you?"

"Of course it's me! Daddy, what the *hell* is wrong with you?"

"I can't believe it," he said, his voice cracking. For the first time, Rachel heard her father cry.

"What?" Rachel asked, desperate.

"We . . . we thought you were dead."

"Dead! What are you talking about? I just got back from vacation." She heard the shuffling of the phone then heard her mother's voice.

"Rachel, honey? Is it you, is it really you?" she asked frantically.

"Of course it's me! I'm fine. I'm certainly not dead! Who told you that?"

Her mother started crying hysterically and was trying to say something through her sobs, but Rachel couldn't make out the words.

"Mom, slow down, I can't understand you."

"We—we thought you were dead, baby," her mother managed to say through her uncontrollable weeping.

"My god! Why would you think that?"

"We were told by the police that you had been murdered. We went down to the morgue and identified you ourselves! The girl," she paused and took a deep breath, "looked identical to you. Oh god, we thought it was you lying there. There was no doubt in our mind—"

Rachel cut in. "Told by the police it was me? How can that be?" Rachel asked, feeling dizzy.

"I don't know, but both Daddy and I saw you with our own eyes!"

"How did she die?" Rachel asked, her heart throttling in her chest.

"They think it was the Heartbreak Killer. You know, the one who's been all over the news? They told us your throat had been slashed. We saw it ourselves!"

Terror ran through Rachel's body like a freight train.

There it was. The dream. The dream about her own murder. But none of it made sense.

"Rachel, you need to hurry over here. We need to see you for ourselves!"

"Mom, I gotta go, but I will swing by as soon as I can."

"Oh honey, please hurry. Come right away. I need to see you just to make sure I'm not imagining all this. We were absolutely devastated.

We've both been sitting here absolute wrecks. This is a miracle, a miracle."

"Yes, Mom, it is," Rachel couldn't agree more.

As soon as Anita hung up the phone, she grabbed Carl and squeezed him tighter than she thought humanly possible. He shifted. His body paralyzed. Anita looked up and saw an expression on his face she had never before witnessed.

"What's wrong, Carl? Our baby is OK. It's OK now! Why are you looking at me like that?"

"Anita," he said tentatively. "Think about it. I think we're in real bad trouble."

"Why? Our baby is alive!"

"No, Rachel's not dead, but I think we know who is," he said, his voice shaking.

Anita's tear-stained face fell and then froze. Her eyes widened with panic as the realization came to her. "Oh god, Carl . . . no . . . what are we going to do?"

"I don't know, Anita. I just don't know."

Chapter 27

"Yes, can I speak with Ted Parchelli?" Rachel asked the woman at the police station.

"Who may I ask is calling?" Perma-Hair snarled. Rachel could tell by her voice that it was the same cantankerous woman who always answered the phone at the precinct.

"He's not going to believe you when I tell you this, but this is Rachel Carter. There's been a mix-up in a homicide. He thinks I'm dead, but I'm not. I'm very much alive. It's no joke. Please, it's urgent," Rachel snapped.

"Hang on," Perma-Hair responded like she had another nutcase on the phone. Within seconds, Ted was on the phone.

"Hello?"

"Ted, it's me, Rachel."

There was a pause. "Rachel? What?"

"Yes, there's been some sort of mix-up in the homicide. The girl you found murdered isn't me! It must be some girl who looks a lot like me."

"Well then, she must be your double because everyone, even your parents, identified her as you at the morgue."

"I know, I know. I don't know what's going on either. I can just tell you for sure the murdered girl isn't me. I am very much alive."

"I'll need you to come down to the station immediately to confirm this. I can't take this at face value," he said suspiciously. "I mean, it sounds like you, but I don't know how that could be possible. I mean, your own parents identified you."

"Sure. I'm on my way. I'd also like to see the girl at the morgue, if that's OK. I mean, I'd like to see her for myself."

"What you need to do is get down here immediately."

"I'll be there in about twenty minutes."

Rachel put the exhaust pedal to the floor. She was anxious to see this mystery girl everyone thought was her. She couldn't imagine the scare it put her parents through, not to mention everyone else. She thought of Brett.

Were the dreams she was having about her own murder really a dream about someone else all along? Someone she just thought was herself? Did she have a double out there? Her parents seemed to think so. Ted seemed to think so. It was uncanny. No! In the dream, there was no doubt it was her lying there with her throat slashed. It wasn't someone who just looked like her! She saw her own face! Who is the poor woman at the morgue?

She was inching near eighty in a forty-mile-an-hour speed zone. The light turned red and she screeched to a stop, nearly hitting a pedestrian walking across the crosswalk. The old woman was wearing tattered clothes and looked like a bag lady, pushing her life's possessions around in a grocery cart. She snarled at Rachel as she veered herself and her cart away from Rachel's car.

"C'mon, c'mon!" Rachel screamed out loud. It seemed to be an eternity before the light turned green. When the light finally turned, she blew through the intersection and her speedometer escalated towards eighty again.

Rachel ran into the police station like a bat out of hell. She bypassed Perma-Hair and went straight to Ted's office. Both Ted and Brett were wearing a hole in the ground from their nervous pacing, awaiting her arrival. Out of the two, Rachel couldn't determine whose face turned more white.

"Well, this isn't a joke," Ted said, his eyes wild.

Without a word, Brett's mouth dropped to the floor. Then he sprinted over to her and grabbed her and held her head to his chest. "Thank God, thank God you're OK," he sighed, his anxiety dissipating.

"Here I am, alive and kicking," Rachel said, hugging him back. She felt his body quiver as he held her.

"Well, this is a first. It *is* you," Ted said. "You'd be surprised what cruel jokes some people play, even when it concerns someone else's death."

"Can we go to the morgue? I need to see this woman for myself."

"Yes. You better brace yourself, Rachel. You're not going to believe your eyes either. In fact, it's the woman's eyes that made me have no doubt it was you."

"They're beautiful eyes," Brett chimed in, squeezing Rachel closer to him.

"I know. I know. Everyone tells me they've never seen anyone else with my eye color. People always think I'm fibbing when I tell them I'm not wearing colored contact lenses," she said, batting her eyes at Brett and returning his infectious smile.

A half hour later, they were at the morgue. Rachel stared down at the dead girl. She couldn't believe it. There she was, her perfect replica. There was no difference. Without any hesitation at all, Rachel took the back of her hand and gently glided it along the woman's cold dead face. She felt her heart pounding in her chest and her mouth went dry.

"Something is going on here, Ted," she said, her voice quivering. She couldn't take her eyes off of the girl. Every feature the woman had was identical to her own—her hair, her mouth, her nose, her profile. Yes, she was dead, ashen, gray, cut—but it was her double. There was no question.

"She looks like she could be my identical twin," Rachel said out loud to no one in particular after the coroner lifted her eyelids so

Rachel could see the practically transparent pale blue eyes she shared with her. "It doesn't make sense. I don't have a twin."

"You sure about that?" Ted asked, cocking an eyebrow.

Brett addressed Ted, frustrated. "Come on, Ted. I think if Rachel had a twin sister, she would know it. Don't be ridiculous!" Turning to Rachel, he said, "It's obviously just someone who looks like you."

"Well, I *was* adopted," Rachel said somberly. "But I didn't have a twin."

Just then, Ted's cell phone rang. "Parchelli here," he snapped. "Oh, Monica, glad you called. Yep . . . yep . . . she's standing right in front of me. I can't believe my eyes. She's definitely alive."

Rachel heard Monica's voice on the other end of the line, and then Ted handed her the phone.

"Yes, it's me. I'm alive!" Rachel screeched into the phone.

"Thank God! You had us all in an uproar. We were all so devastated." Monica gasped.

"Well, I guess you're not a world-renowned psychic for nothing. You were right. The girl in my dream wasn't me. You should see her though. She's a spitting image!"

"So I've heard," Monica responded, relieved. "I wonder who she is?"

"I don't know, but looking at her, you would think she were my twin or something. Even I can't believe the resemblance."

"I'm so glad you're OK! Rachel, you don't know how relieved I am."

"Yeah, you and me both," she said then looked up at Ted and Brett. "I think there's a few other people who are relieved as well."

"Have you talked to your parents, do they know?"

"Yes. That's when it all came down. I called them to let them know I was back from vacation, and they acted like they were talking to a ghost. Actually, they thought it was a crank call," Rachel said, laughing.

"Well, this shouldn't be a surprise to me. I had no doubt you were safe, but when Ted told me about the murder, I was mortified and confused. I admit, I did question myself."

"I'm sorry I doubted you, Monica. I'm so sorry."

"Nothing to be sorry about, I'm just glad you're safe."

"I'll call you later, OK?"

"OK. I'm glad I spoke to you. I can finally breathe again."

"Me too."

Rachel handed the phone back to Ted.

"So, Ted, who is this woman?" Monica asked.

"She's Jane Doe for now. We've got some work to do to identify her. No one has called in with a missing person's report on her."

"We need to find out. It's a mystery."

"Yes it is. It's more than a mystery. I've never seen anything like this before."

"Keep me posted."

"Sure thing," Ted said and clicked off his phone and placed it back on his belt clip. Looking up at Rachel, he said. "So now it's time to find out who this girl is. You sure you don't have a sister?"

"Not that I know of. I mean, like I said, I was adopted, but my parents never said anything about a sister."

Brett, still holding on to Rachel for dear life, chimed in, "It's probably just someone who looks like you. I mean, I know it's weird, but some people say that everyone has a double somewhere. I'm sure she's not related to you." Ted just looked at Brett with a "how-dumb-can-you-be" expression. There was no doubt there had to be at least some sort of relation.

"If I had a sister, my parents must have known that when they adopted me," Rachel said, confused. "The adoption agency would have told them. I am going to see them now. If there is any relation, they have a lot of explaining to do."

"You check with them, and in the meantime, I've got to get to work on my end," Ted said, cradling his face in one hand as he looked down at the dead girl.

Chapter 28

The whole situation seemed so surreal to Rachel. A sister? It couldn't be. If true, and her parents had known all this time, it would be such a monumental betrayal. Why wouldn't they have told her? Rachel's head was spinning—it was beyond comprehension to accept such a blow. If she hadn't seen the girl lying there, a perfect replica of herself, she wouldn't have believed it either. Rachel started to feel anger building in her. *If I did have a twin, why didn't Mom and Dad tell me?* she questioned herself. Her mind was swimming. Her thoughts were all jumbled up, entangled in each other like a puzzle. The pieces just didn't fit.

There were too many questions that she needed to ask her parents. If the dead girl was her sister, then why didn't they adopt both of them? Her mother was adamant about taking both the twin foster boys. Maybe they didn't even know she had a twin. Maybe her sister had already been adopted out by someone else before her parents adopted her. If not, keeping such a huge secret from her all these years just seemed so out character for her parents, whom she adored and trusted. If they had known and just never told her, it was as if her entire life had been one big lie. Were the two people she trusted the most not who she thought they were? She was grasping for any reason to reconcile this devastation.

When Rachel walked up to her parents' door, she realized that, just like Monica's door had been, it was the only thing that separated her from the truth. When Anita opened the door, she grabbed Rachel and held her tight. "Thank God," Anita said. Carl came running to the door, and when he saw Rachel, he broke down in tears again. It was so strange to see this huge, strong man, who'd always been so tough and stoic, bawl like a baby.

Rachel looked at both her parents for a few seconds completely tongue tied, not knowing what to say in spite of the rehearsed speech and the barrage of questions she had. *Had this mother and this father whom she'd known all her life betrayed her? Were they people she really didn't know at all?*

Anita felt the tension in her daughter, and her cheer soon changed to concern. Worry emerged on her face. Still tongue tied, Rachel looked at the only parents she had ever known with tears streaming down her face.

Carl took his daughter as if she were a small child and lifted her in through the house and sat her down on the living room couch.

Fear surged through her. How was this conversation going to end? Yes, she had a sister, and her parents had lied to her all these years? Or no, she didn't have a sister and no one knew who the woman at the morgue was? Or she had a sister, but her parents knew nothing about her?

Rachel could see the worried look on her parents' faces. They sat there, terrified. "Mom, Dad," Rachel said, looking from one parent to the other. "I just came from the morgue and I have something I need to ask you." She saw both her parents visibly brace themselves as if Rachel was about to reveal a bombshell. They hung on her every word.

Rachel's mouth was as dry as the Sahara Desert, and she was worried that her question may come out silent, just like in her dreams. When she did speak, her voice came out shaking, but it was loud and clear. "Did I have a twin?"

Anita and Carl exchanged a worried look. The secret had been exposed. Anita looked down and put her head in her hands, and that said it all.

The shudder that flooded through Rachel carried a myriad of emotion—anger, confusion, betrayal. "How could you? I had a right to know!"

"Dear, your dad and I—"

Rachel cut her off. "So I do . . . *excuse me, I did* . . . have a sister!" Rachel yelled out angrily. "Why didn't you tell me?"

"Rachel," her father said frantically. "Your mother and I did what we felt was best at the time."

"Best?" Rachel's face contorted in pain. "You did what you felt was best? Best for who? You two?"

Anita looked up at Rachel with guilt exuding out of every pore in her body. "The truth is that we couldn't take you both."

"So you just decided that it would be OK to tear me away from my sister—my identical twin sister?"

"Look, Rachel," Carl cleared his throat. "Your mother and I were going to tell you at one time, but then decided it would be best if you never knew."

"Why? Why would you do that?" Rachel stood up, shaking her head, turning away from them. Turning back to face them, she was full of rage. "I could've had a relationship with her! She was my sister! You had no right to deny me that! I trusted you both my whole life. I . . ." Rachel paused. "That's what kids do, they trust their parents! You were both my foundation for my life. You lied to me, you both betrayed me—my whole life has been a lie! I had a sister—a sister! You knew I had one and you never told me? And now . . . now it's too late. She's dead!"

Rachel was shaking her head in disgust. "You could care less about what happened to my own twin, my *identical* twin. The thing is—I could've accepted it if you had told me from the start! It would probably have been hard, but I would've gotten through it. I could have looked for her and maybe gotten to know her. Now it's too late."

Rachel grabbed her purse off the couch and headed for the door. Both Carl and Anita jumped up from where they were sitting. Anita rushed toward her and grabbed her shoulder. "Rachel, please . . ."

Rachel shoved her mother's hand off her shoulder. "Do not touch me!" she said viciously. Anita tentatively removed her hand.

"Why? Why? Why?" Rachel cried hysterically.

Before Carl could even reach his daughter, she was out the door.

Brett held her tightly. "It's OK, Rach. I know everything seems like it is falling apart right now, but it's all going to work out."

"I just don't understand how my parents could do that to me," she cried, resting her head on his shoulder.

"I don't know. Back then, they must've had their reasons. Try to look at it that way. Try not to be angry with them."

"How can I not be angry?" Rachel lifted her head to look at him.

He used his thumb to dry a freshly fallen tear from her face. "I know it doesn't make sense right now, but try to forgive them. They love you with all their heart."

"I just wish they had been straight with me. I could've taken it even if it meant being separated from her."

"It doesn't make sense, I know. Maybe they felt that you wouldn't have been able to live separately from her—especially because she was more than a sister, she was your twin," Brett said, kissing the top of her head.

"Maybe that's because identical twins *shouldn't be* separated!" Rachel said bitterly. "I should've known about her and she should've known about me. Period."

"I agree with you, Rachel," Brett said, he tucked a piece of hair behind her ear then softly caressed her cheek.

"The funny thing is, is that I've always felt an emptiness in my heart. A hollowness I never could understand," Rachel said, rubbing her hand over her heart. "And then when I met the twin foster boys, I really felt something missing. Something familiar . . . but not there."

"That's probably natural," Brett said. "Twins are connected in ways that other siblings aren't, I'm sure."

"Yes. It's a tragedy that she and I were deprived of that special bond. That's what I'm so mad about. Now . . . ," Rachel said, burying her head back into Brett's shoulder, "she's dead, and we'll never be able to have a relationship or even get to know each other."

"I know, baby. I would give anything to change that for you."

"I just don't know if I will ever forgive my parents," Rachel whispered.

"You need to forgive them. Harboring anger is bad for you. Not forgiving someone is like drinking your own poison. Just concentrate on how loving they have been to you your whole life. I'm sure they didn't keep it a secret to hurt you. They must have felt it was the best decision to not let you know, at least at the time. As you got older, maybe it just seemed too awkward to bring it up. Besides, what could they do about it then?"

"I'm sure they did have their reasons, but it feels like a huge betrayal to me now."

"I know. I don't completely understand it either."

"Well, I guess the silver lining in this whole mess is that my dreams make sense now. All along, the girl in my dream wasn't me. It was my identical twin sister."

"That's right. Although it is horrible that you never knew about her, at least we know *you* are now safe," Brett said, looking into her with loving gray eyes. "I'm so happy you are here with me."

"Me too," she said, smiling at him.

He leaned down and kissed her gently on the mouth. She turned her body toward him and kissed him back. He took her head in his hands and kissed her harder. She felt his warm body against hers, every muscle tensing. It felt so natural to be with him and to be sharing such intimacy.

He broke from the kiss and took her hand in his and led her to his bedroom then turned and closed the door. When he turned back around, Rachel could see the fire burning in his eyes. She watched him slowly walk toward her. Butterflies were starting to churn within her. She couldn't remember a time when she wanted a man more—not even Jack.

He started unbuttoning her blouse—his hands moving gracefully from one button down to the next. After he unbuttoned the last one, he placed his hands on her shoulders and gently slid her shirt off. He reached behind her and unhooked her bra, allowing her breasts to fall free. Standing up, he slowly pushed her back onto the bed then reached for his belt buckle. Without taking his eyes off hers, he undressed. She was drawn to how beautiful his body was, muscular and lean, and wanting. When he was done, he lowered down and kissed her. Rachel felt the burn rush through her body and she knew then she wanted him—all of him.

She relished every sensation of Brett's hands, his mouth. Her breath caught as he cupped her breasts. Rachel heard herself moan from the pleasure building in her body. He slowly continued down, exploring her body with his tongue. When he got down to the top of her pants, he seductively looked up at her. "Are you OK with this?"

"Absolutely," she replied, licking her lips.

"So am I. What it is about the third date?" Brett asked in a sultry voice and winked at her.

He slid her pants down and brushed his face across the red patch of panty. It had been so long since she had made love—not since Jack. The physical and emotional connection she experienced with Jack paled in comparison to what she was feeling now with Brett.

Brett drank up the hint of her rose-scented perfume. His bare muscular arms flexed as he slid on top of her. He stroked her hair with his hands, his face next to hers. She felt his stubble gently rub against her face.

"Rachel, you are so beautiful," he whispered into her ear, gently kissing the lobe. His breath was hot and quickening. He wanted to consume her, all of her. His lips and tongue gently glided across her neck and down her shoulders. His bare skin against hers made her feel as if they were one and always had been.

It was Brett's first time with Rachel, and he wanted to take it slow, pleasure her, take pleasure himself in seeing her surrender herself to him.

Chapter 29

Tanya Sullivan's knees buckled at the sight of her best friend lying on the gurney. Her surroundings were the epitome of death—the stainless steel cabinets and counters, the bright lights, the surgical instruments, the smell. Death. She had only seen one other dead person before—her mother, and she had been expecting that. It was horrible to see her mother with a disease-ravaged body, but it was worse to see her best friend lying there with a ravaged body caused by a death so senseless . . . so savage . . .

"I'm so sorry, Kristin," she said, hesitantly reaching over to touch Kristin's face. It was as cold as ice. Her best friend was dead.

"Hey, Rachel, Ted here."

"Hi, Ted, have you gotten any word yet on who our 'Jane Doe' is?" Rachel asked anxiously.

"Yes, that's why I'm calling you. Her name is Kristin Townsend. Apparently, she was an exotic dancer at a place called Honeysuckles. She lived in Renton. Ever heard of her?"

"No, how did you find out that's who it is?"

"Her roommate, Tanya Sullivan, came forward. Said Kristin hadn't come home for a few days."

"Did she go by the morgue and identify her?"

"Yes. She made a positive identification," Parchelli said and paused. "Look, I don't know how you feel about this, but Tanya would like to meet with you."

"Really? So you told her about me?" Rachel responded, her heart stopped.

"Yes. I hope that was OK. I have her phone number if you'd like to meet with her."

Rachel sat across from Tanya at Joe's Diner. She was a tall brunette with thick eyeliner that swooshed up at the corners of her brown eyes, giving her an exotic look. Pale pink lipstick. Slightly overweight, she wore faded jeans and a long-sleeved yellow sweater. She had a diamond chip that pierced one nostril.

"What was she like?" Rachel asked, her voice tight in her throat.

"She was a special girl, my best friend," Tanya said quietly. "She was someone I could always count on. I trusted her, she trusted me. In this world, that's pretty rare."

"Had you been friends for a long time?" Rachel asked curiously.

"I've known her since she was about seventeen. That's when she started walking the streets with me. We became really close. Always there for each other, ya know?" Tanya said.

"Walking the streets?" Rachel asked, confused.

"Yeah, hooking. That's what we do . . . that's what she used to do," Tanya said flatly. "But she had just recently gotten into dancing."

Rachel was taken aback. *A prostitute?* Ted hadn't given her this information. Maybe he didn't know. Rachel was stunned but tried not to show it or pass judgment. That would only hinder the conversation, and she needed to keep Tanya talking.

"We both had it pretty rough growing up," Tanya said, shaking her head, the diamond in her nose gleaming from the light.

"In what way?" Rachel asked curiously, taking a sip of her coffee.

"In her case, it was alcohol. She didn't have a problem with it, but both her parents did. They took it out on her," Tanya shrugged. "That's why she ran away at such a young age. That's why she ended up in prostitution, ya know," Tanya said defensively. "It was *their* fault. She had to eat."

"You said she had just started dancing?" Rachel asked.

"Yeah, she had just started as an exotic dancer at Honeysuckles . . . It's on Pacific Highway South, down by the airport," Tanya said, nervously playing with her left earring.

"Wow, the same strip the Green River Killer took his victims from."

"Yeah . . . dangerous place to be," Tanya said. "Prostitution is dangerous. That was one of the reasons she wanted to get out of it. You never know what crazy person you may end up with. I've met a few looney tunes in the past."

Tanya looked at Rachel strangely. "Why are you looking at me like that?" Rachel asked.

"I just can't believe how much you look like her. I mean, with most twins, even if they are identical, there is usually *some* difference in how they look," Tanya said, shaking her head. "But with you two . . . there is nothing different. I mean, it's like I'm seeing a ghost. It's kind of eerie, ya know. I mean, I don't mean that in a bad way, I—"

"I know what you mean. I saw her too," Rachel cut in. "I didn't see her alive, obviously, but I could see that we looked the same."

"I'm going to miss her," Tanya said, her eyes starting to tear up.

"Do you have any pictures of her?" Rachel asked.

"I do have one," Tanya replied, reaching for her purse. She pulled out her wallet and fished out a small tattered picture strip. "Here's one of us together. It was taken at one of those coin-operated photo booths. You can see three different expressions of her."

Rachel gently took the strip of pictures and analyzed it. In one, Kristin was smiling; in the next one, she had a silly surprised look on her face; and in the last one, she was sticking her tongue out.

"Those were happier times," Tanya said somberly. "That was taken shortly after she ran away from home. Right after she started hooking."

Rachel kept staring at the picture. It was surreal. It looked like she was staring back at herself. "If only I had known her. I feel like there's been such a loss. I wish I had known her."

"I think a lot of people judged her wrong because of what she did to survive, but they didn't know her heart. I did. She had no choice. She was trying to change her life. She told her pimp that she just couldn't hustle anymore."

"Had you lived together long?" Rachel asked.

"Yeah, for a couple of years," Tanya answered. "When she didn't come home that night and I still hadn't heard from her the next day . . . I knew something bad had happened, so I called the police." Tanya's lip started to quiver.

"Here," Rachel said, taking a napkin out of the dispenser and handing it to her. "I'm sorry."

Tanya dabbed her eyes. "She had such a sweet heart. I mean, she would've given me the shirt off her back if she thought I needed it. I don't understand why this had to happen to her. She, out of anyone, didn't deserve this."

"Nobody deserves to die like she did," Rachel said sadly.

"You would've loved her," Tanya sobbed.

Rachel reached across the table and placed her hand on top of Tanya's. "I'm sure I would have. I wish I would've had the chance to."

"Kristin never mentioned having a sister. I doubt she knew," Tanya said.

"That makes two of us. Doesn't sound like her parents told her she was a twin either."

"That seems odd to me. I mean, why wouldn't your parents or her parents have said something about it?" Tanya asked, taking a sip of ice water.

"That's a good question. I confronted my parents about it, and they told me they just thought it was best I didn't know . . . for whatever reason."

"I don't know . . . that just doesn't seem right. Why wouldn't they want you to know?"

"I was pretty pissed off at them about that."

"Yeah, I would be too," Tanya said, using her spoon to spin the ice around in her glass.

"I'm just glad I know now. Not that it makes any difference now . . . but still."

"I'm sure she would have liked to have known you also," Tanya said smiling.

Chapter 30

The three of them sat around the kitchen table and stared at each other silently. Awkwardness shrouded the atmosphere like a heavy cloak.

"Just tell me why," were the first words spoken out of Rachel's mouth.

Carl shot a quick glance at Anita, scrambling for support. "Rachel, we never did feel right about adopting just you, but we really didn't have much of a choice."

"What do you mean you didn't have a choice?" Rachel snapped.

"At that time," Carl continued, clearing his throat to buy time. "We couldn't take you both. Quite frankly, we couldn't afford it."

"Didn't the adoption agency want you to take both of us?" Rachel asked on the verge of tears, her voice quivering.

"Yes, they did," Anita chimed in quietly. "But, like Daddy said, we couldn't afford two babies."

"Then why didn't you take another baby, one that wasn't a twin?" Rachel said, still not understanding.

"Honey, there weren't any other little girls available . . . besides, you were so beautiful. You were just perfect for us," Anita, also teary eyed, explained.

"But you knew it wasn't the right thing to do. You shouldn't have split us up. I mean, you yourself told me that you knew it would be wrong to split up the foster twins boys," Rachel said, darting her eyes back and forth between her mom and dad.

"Rachel," her father said. "We did what we had to do."

"But it wasn't right! You ripped us apart!"

"Honey," Anita said. "We were told that there was another couple who wanted your sister, and we were assured they were good people."

"Well, you may want to know that they weren't good people," Rachel said snidely. "Her parents abused her—they were drunks!"

Her parents looked shocked. "We had no idea that was the case. We trusted the adoption agency to place her into a loving family," Carl said.

"You shouldn't have trusted them. Because of this whole situation, Kristin was put into an abusive family and lived a hard life. You should've taken her," Rachel reprimanded.

"Looking back now, that probably would've been the best. But like we said, we figured your sister would be placed in a good home. It's the responsibility of the adoption agency to screen people. They wouldn't have placed her with those people if they thought they would abuse her," Anita said, shifting uncomfortably in her chair.

Rachel's voice iced over. "If you would've taken her she would've had a good home!"

Anita and Carl looked at each other sheepishly, wondering which one of them was going to speak next.

Rachel sneered, "Besides all that, you had no right to take her from me. She was my twin sister, my identical twin sister!"

"Rachel," her mother said in quiet desperation. "We made a mistake, and if we could take back time, we would've found a way to take her too."

Rachel's voice constricted. "Did you know she ended up living on the streets? That she was a prostitute? She had a horrible life!"

Carl and Anita were shocked again by her words. They had no idea.

"Yeah, that's right. She ended up a prostitute!" Rachel seethed.

"We didn't know," Carl said sympathetically.

"No, honey, we didn't know that," Anita said.

The tears started to flow as Rachel just looked down at the table.

"Please, Rachel, please forgive us," Carl pleaded. "We know now that we made a mistake—we should've taken her also and just found a way to afford it. We now see the importance of keeping twins together. We've learned that through watching the foster boys."

"It wasn't right," Anita agreed. "We are sorry."

Anita reached out to touch Rachel's hand, but Rachel snapped her hand back. "Please don't, Mom, just don't."

Anita slid her hand back and instead grasped Carl's hand. She looked at Carl with a world of grief painted on her face. He gave her a reassuring squeeze with his hand.

"It's bad enough to have been deprived of a relationship with her, but why didn't you tell me about her?" Rachel asked desperately.

"We thought it would just make it harder on you, Rachel," her father explained.

"So you just decided to lie to me by not telling me?" Rachel looked at him with tears staining her face.

"You were such a happy baby," Anita said. "We didn't think it would be the right decision to tell you and just have you wonder about her all your life."

"So you betrayed me twice," Rachel said, narrowing her eyes. "First, you ripped me away from her. And second, you never told me about her."

Rachel stood up and started pacing the hardwood floor. "So you made the decision to foster both of the twin boys because you felt guilty about what you did to me, right?" she snarled.

Anita couldn't answer her. Rachel's words stung like a slap in the face.

"We made a mistake, Rachel," Carl said. "We can't take it back now. All we can do is ask you to forgive us. Please."

"I don't know. It's going to take me time," Rachel said, shaking her head.

"We understand that, baby," Anita soothed. "We just want you to know we didn't do it to hurt you—or hurt Kristin."

Rachel sat down again and just looked down at her hands, not knowing what to say.

"You take as much time as you need. Just know that we love you with all our hearts and always have. I guess we just thought we were protecting you by not telling you about your twin. We worried about the pain it may have caused you. And . . . like I said, we were wrong. We should've told you about her."

"Yes, you were wrong. The thing is that, I've always had an emptiness in my heart that I never could explain. Now, I know what that emptiness was. It was a place for Kristin," Rachel said, pain tugging at her soul.

"Unfortunately, that's an emptiness that your mother and I can't fill," Carl said. "I would do anything to fill that if I could."

"It's too late now," Rachel said, her anger dissipating to sadness. "She's gone forever."

Anita began to weep. Carl got out of his chair to hold her.

Rachel watched his dad comfort his mother, and a wave of sadness washed over her.

"Mom, Dad, I do love you both, and I want to forgive you," Rachel said. "I just need time."

Her mother and father looked at her, now both with tears in their eyes. "I hope so, honey—I hope so," her dad said, choking on his words. Her mother was too upset to speak but shook her head in agreement.

"I will," Rachel sighed. "I will. I just have to mourn the loss."

Her father walked over to Rachel and hugged her. To her surprise, she was able to hug him back. She then reached out and took her mother's hand in her own.

Chapter 31

Randall sat in the courtroom with his head hung low. He took the beating one after the other as the victims' family members slung words at him like knives. Lisa's parents were uncontrollable with their scathing accusations while Danielle's parents were quiet and forgiving. Rachel couldn't understand how they could forgive him. How do you forgive someone who has altered your world forever? Someone who has taken away something priceless and irreplaceable? How could they find it in their heart to let those feelings dissolve so quickly? She considered herself a forgiving person, but this? No way. She hadn't even grown up with Kristin, and she would never forgive him for murdering her.

"Randall, I will never forget what you have done to my family," Danielle's father said with a quivering voice. "You have taken from me, and everyone in my family, something that can never be returned. My daughter, my precious little girl, is gone, taken from all of us by your own hands." He went on. "A daughter, a sister, a granddaughter—we have all suffered incredible pain. But for me to stand here and tell you what a horrible monster you are wouldn't do anyone any good. I am not a vengeful man, and neither is my family. We are all strong in our Christian faith and Jesus would want us, just as he did, to forgive those who do wrong—even in such a horrific way." When the man turned to leave the podium, his knees buckled, and several people from the aisles rushed to his aid to help him up.

Lisa Connelly's mother wasn't so forgiving. Randall kept his head down. "Randall, you are a monster, a twisted soul. You are a demon and you need to go back to hell where you belong! How could you take my baby from me? Look into her innocence and murder her in the grisly way that you did? The man before me forgives you, but I don't, and I never will. May you rot in hell and burn for eternity, and you will Randall, you will. But before you are cast down to hell, may you have to face my baby and explain to her why you did what you did. If my beautiful daughter has a say—if she can tell you the horror and fear you brought to her in her last minutes of life—she would want you to burn too. May you suffer, suffer, much worse than what my daughter did. If there is a God, may he see that justice and cast you into the fire for all eternity." She was so angry, her voice was shaking. "You are . . ." Before she could get the rest of the sentence out, her husband walked up and gently led her back to her chair. He had a good grip on her, but still she turned back towards Randall. "You are the devil!"

Rachel waited patiently as her turn to speak neared. She was last, and there was a reason for it. Randall had not recognized her during the trial because she had sat in the back. She had wrapped her hair up in a baseball cap and had worn shaded sunglasses. She didn't want him to see her—not during the trial. He was in for the fright of his life and he didn't even know it.

Rachel walked up to the podium. Randall continued to look at the floor. She took off her hat, allowing her hair to fall loose. She took off her sunglasses, and her pale blue eyes glared at Randall. He deserved the full effect—the horror, the fear, and everything else that would come with seeing what he would probably assume was a ghost of someone who he had killed.

"Randall, I need you to look at me," Rachel said softly. He refused, keeping his eyes glued to the floor.

"Randall, please, I need you to look up at me."

Slowly, he raised his head. The terror on his face was indescribable. He reeled back in his chair—the chains on his feet getting caught in the legs of the chair when he tried to stand.

"Please, please . . . you're dead. You're dead. Where—where . . . why are you here?"

Rachel said nothing. She just stared him down with her eyes—eyes that he had once seen the life drain from.

"Please, please stop looking at me! You're dead!"

"Order in the courtroom, order in the court room," the judge said, sternly pounding his gavel on the podium.

Randall tried to flee the court room. It took three people to prevent him from doing so. He finally sat back down in his chair. He put his head down so he didn't have to look into Rachel's face. He didn't want to look into the same eyes as someone he had killed.

"That's right, Randall. I'm the ghost of Kristin Townsend. I'm sure you remember her," Rachel said smugly. "The dancer? You slaughtered her."

With that being said, the entire court room erupted with confusion. "Order in the court." The judge was continuing to try to control the court room. "Miss Carter, please proceed. But get to the point. You are causing a major disruption with your nebulous confrontation."

"Yes, Your Honor. I apologize."

"Randall. I am not Kristin, but I am someone very close to her. My name is Rachel. I'm her identical twin sister. When you killed her, Randall, you killed a part of me. I ask myself every day *why*, why you would do such a thing—not only to my sister, but to all of the poor innocent girls and their families. You are a sick, sick person. Though I think you should be put to death, there is a part of me that wishes you could sit in your tiny cell for the rest of your life and think about what you have done to us all—and be haunted forever by all the women whose lives you stole and stole so young. I hope you live in misery for the rest of your days for what you did to those women and all these people," she said, looking back and panning the victims' families with her hand. "And I want you to think about what you ripped out of my heart." Randall didn't look up again at her, but tears pooled on the table he was sitting at, and his breathing was labored.

Chapter 32

Randall held the picture of his mother tightly to his chest—the one thing the guards allowed him to take with him to the death chamber. With every step he took, the clanking of the chains on his feet echoed through death row, reminding and terrifying the other inmates that someday they may walk the same path. It was different for Randall. He had refused any appeals and actually fought to expedite his execution. His eyes were closed and he was mumbling, as if in prayer. He wasn't praying to God as many might presume, but rather to his mother. In his mind, his execution would show her that he was willing to lay down his life for her love.

He didn't appear nervous or scared—relief was more the expression that spread across his broad face. Once in the room, the guards reluctantly took the picture from Randall and placed it on a shelf that would allow him to see it through his dying process. They then helped him up onto the table, and he spread his enormous arms out so they could secure them with the straps, then his legs. He was strapped down without any resistance, and he actually welcomed the lethal fluid that would soon run through his veins. Once he was tightly secured, the curtain to the viewing room opened.

Rachel actually winced at the sight. Randall was stretched out on the table, reminding her of how Jesus Christ looked on the cross. Ironically, Randall too was making the ultimate sacrifice—not for all humanity as Jesus did, but rather for his mother's love.

A guard asked him if he had any last words. A few seconds passed as if Randall was deep in thought as to how he was going to say what he needed to. "To my mother," he said, choking back tears as he looked at her picture, "I hope you can forgive me now." He paused, just looking at her, and then shifted his eyes to the double-mirrored barrier—the only thing that separated him from those whose lives he had altered forever. "To all of you, I hope that one day you will realize that I am not the monster you think I am—I am a kind and gentle man, and that is the truth." Rachel shivered when Randall's eyes locked with hers. It was as if he was talking directly to her. She questioned for a moment whether he could actually see her through the window.

Randall turned his head back to his mother's picture. He no longer saw hatred and disdain—instead, her eyes looked at him kindly, lovingly. No longer was her mouth spitting acid—instead, she was smiling at him in a warm and soothing way.

The guard pushed the first lever down, prompting the fluid to drain into Randall's vein. Randall heard his mother whisper into his ear, *'The girls you murdered are now here with me, and like me, they are no longer beautiful.'* The second lever was pushed down. Randall heard his mother whisper into his other ear, *'Now you are sacrificing your own life for me.'* The third and final lever was pushed down. It seemed to Rachel that the fluid from that portal flowed down the tube much slower—almost as if it had a consciousness all its own, reluctant to take this man's life no matter how heinous his crimes had been. '*Randall, my sweet child, I can now forgive you,*' were the last words Randall Metzgar heard deep within the remnants of his consciousness. The intolerable screaming had finally quieted. His mother's face faded from his vision for the last time. Rachel wondered if Randall really did believe that he was a good person, but one who had been driven to the unthinkable by a force outside himself. He didn't look like a monster now. Rather, he looked more like someone who was finally at peace—free from the torment that consumed him for most of his life.

Rachel heard soft cries from some of the people around her—most supporting each other to exit the room, heads bowed. No one felt joy. A strong wave of sadness settled in Rachel's gut. An eye for an eye wouldn't make those victims come back—and no justice, however final, would ever allow the pain to subside for those families. That pain will linger forever. However, the pain for Randall Metzgar was gone. He was dead.

Chapter 33

Rachel crawled underneath the comforter and into Brett's arms.

"I'm so glad it's over," she said, sighing.

"Yes. No more worries. I told you I would keep you safe," Brett said with a crooked smile.

Rachel closed her eyes and rested her head down on Brett's chest. The rhythmic sound of his heartbeat lulled her into a deep sleep.

She walked toward the woman, leaving footprints in her wake on the grainy, wet sand. The voice of Mother Nature rang in her ears with every crashing wave, reminding her that some things cannot and are not meant to be altered. Just like her connection with Kristin. Even the secret that she had been born as an only child could not alter the natural bond that she had with her twin. That pull, that tug on her heart she had felt her whole life now made sense. She realized that emptiness in her heart had always been a sacred place—a place for Kristin.

As the two came closer, one face became the reflection of the other. Rachel stared in awe at her sister. Everything, all their features, had been chiseled by the same hand. Kristin smiled warmly at Rachel. Rachel tried to return the smile, but tears just welled in her eyes. Kristin reached over and gently wiped a tear that had fallen down Rachel's face. Finally, when Rachel was able to speak, she did so with a voice Kristin had shared. "I am so, so sorry," Rachel's voice broke into a whimper.

"You have nothing to be sorry about," Kristin said, reaching for her and pulling Rachel into her arms. Rachel took comfort in finally being able to feel her twin's body next to hers—their heart beating as one.

"You have set me free," Kristin whispered into Rachel's ear. The warmth of her breath flowed through Rachel's body like a comforting caress. "I reached out for you, and you heard me—I pleaded for you to see me in your dreams—to hear me in your dreams. You heard my desperate cries—cries I knew that only you would be able to hear." Kristin pulled back and touched Rachel's face.

"You heard me because we are one—we always have been. So don't be sad, Rachel. Everything is right now—you made it right for me, and I thank you for that," Kristin soothed. "Now I can go—I can go in peace."

"Please—please don't go. I just found you—I don't want to lose you again," Rachel cried, pulling Kristin back into her arms.

"You are not losing me. Just as it has always been, I will be with you. I will be right here," she said, putting her warm hand over Rachel's heart and then placed Rachel's hand over her own. "You will feel me, just as I will feel you. That empty feeling in our soul that we have both felt our whole lives is filled now—it will never haunt us again."

"Please, please don't go." Kristin just smiled warmly at her. She knew that Rachel did not, could not, yet understand, but she was comforted in knowing that someday she would.

Kristin held Rachel's face again and gently kissed her on the cheek. She slowly pulled away. "I will always be with you," Kristin soothed. "Always . . ."

Rachel felt the warm love of her sister resonate through her body—the love she knew would never leave her. Although the tears continued to flow, she knew it was time to let go. She smiled as she watched her sister walk slowly away into the early morning fog until she became one with it.